OLD DEMON AND THE SEA WITCH

WELCOME TO HELL #10 ~ HELL CRUISE
ADVENTURE

EVE LANGLAIS

SHAX: HAVE YOU READ THE BOOK, HOW TO TRAIN YOUR GOBLINS? DON'T. IT'S A LIE!

THE LITTLE GREEN bastard fired a first edition of *Pet Sematary*, signed by the King himself, at me. I winced as it hit a bookcase and flopped open to the ground, the pages bent.

"What do you think you're doing?" I roared, appalled at the travesty.

The goblin stuck out his tongue and grabbed a worn but enjoyable romantic story about a demon and his witch. Based on a true story, and a favorite of the staff.

The bastard wound his arm back, ready to toss.

I shoved up my sleeves and prepared to catch. It wouldn't be the first time.

Once more, goblins had snuck into Hell's epic library. It used to be known as the Ashurbanipal, but that was when it was on the Earth plane. Back when I was still kind of human. Before the incident.

With the Ashurbanipal in peril, the librarians at the time, including me, had made a deal with the devil. I got a pair of horns and an extended lifespan. Lucifer got to boast about owning the most extensive library anywhere, and I got to deal with stupid shit like leather-parchment-eating worms and goblins. Neither of which had any respect for the literary word.

And where there was one...

Another book almost clocked me in the head. *War and No Peace*, the alternate ending that added a few hundred additional pages. It would have hurt if it'd landed.

I glared, about all I could do until the library acolytes arrived with the lassos. Good thing our last batch of recruits had been practicing.

People often made the mistake of assuming that librarians were meek scholars with the muscle tone of a human centenarian. Maybe on Earth, but here in the Pit, working the library meant staying fit. Because Hell's library didn't give up its knowledge easily. Bringing it to Hell imbued it with certain challenges. Now, it required quick wits and agile strength to find what you were looking for. The deaths of those who failed probably explained the lack of interest in reading.

The funniest were those who assumed they could cockily enter and do the job of a guardian of the stacks. They didn't believe us when we told them that magic was forbidden inside the library, as were candles—any sort of flame, actually. Sharp-edged objects, even letter openers, had to remain outside the guarded doors. There were some priceless books in here. Irreplaceable ones that could never, *ever* have a copy. Some could not be read by anyone. Some knowledge should remain hidden, but never be destroyed. The library existed to protect wisdom and history.

Anything that might possibly damage a book found itself held outside the doors. At times it was a wonder anyone made it through the powerful magnet that yanked at your flesh as if it would strip out your teeth and bones.

Yet it somehow couldn't stop goblins. Nor the dragon that decided to squat on the *Dungeons and Dragons* section. But we let her have that hoard mostly because we kept the Salvatore books elsewhere.

I ducked before a sudden volley of books—fired by more than one green goblin—could rain on me. It required some fast footwork to leap, grab, tuck a book before flipping to snare another and another. I was a veritable acrobat, catching all the paperbacks before they could land.

Except for one.

The original *Wizard of Oz* manuscript by L. Frank Baum, a first draft handwritten with all the dark, yummy bits before they got edited out to become the modern-day classic. It landed hard enough to snap the binder holding all the loose sheets. They spilled onto the floor.

The goblins, a chattering sort, fell silent. Did they hear the anger ticking inside of me?

Thump. Thump. Thump. One by one, I placed the books I'd managed to save on the table.

"Ergh blag?" The goblin closest to me appeared apprehensive.

With good reason. Because there were some lines even they knew to never cross.

Jerod, a student of mine, arrived with a lasso. Out of breath, and like an idiot, he ran right into the middle of the problem.

But the goblins ignored him to watch me. I held out my hand. The lasso hit my palm.

There was a squeal as the little bastards split, racing through the stacks. As if they could escape.

I twirled the lasso, whipping it out, the circle

rotating, nice and tight. I would have to go hunting, and the aisles didn't leave much room.

I tracked down the first one in the dead end for novels that never made it to market. For example, we had a whole shelf of stories by an author written while being kept prisoner by an avid fan. He died in captivity, and the reader hoarded the books written under extreme duress until Lucifer came to get her soul and she traded them for a spot in Heaven.

Rumor had it she'd kidnapped an angel. The one who'd helped the Christians write their Bible. I couldn't wait to get my hands on that book.

The goblin I tracked hovered mid-shelf, clinging with its gouging claws to the scratchable wood. The bookcase should have been made of something more durable, but the devil liked the look of it.

So did I, but I liked to bust his balls and proffer suggestions that we replace it with industrial metal shelving. I just hoped he never realized I mind-screwed him, or we could end up with a very ware-house look rather than a cozy library.

The creature dared to pull out a volume and wag it. I gave him my sternest look. "I can be nice about this." I eyed the spinning lasso. "Or not."

The thrown tome said not. No remorse filled me as the noose soared and landed around the goblin. He flailed and squawked. I tightened the rope, yanked him towards me, and spun it rapidly until he was bobble-eyed, staring at me from a rope cocoon.

I held out my hand without looking. Someone wisely gave me another rope. I hunted down the rest of the goblins, bundling them one by one. Some of my acolytes managed to snare a few.

There was only one left. He sat in the baby section, surrounded by books about raising them, corrupting them, the things to expect, the crazy mommy stories never published because infanticide was frowned upon.

The beast eyed me with black orbs that didn't blink. He softened his expression, made his mouth tremble. He appeared innocent and childlike. I could feel my acolytes around me weakening.

They'd learn.

I said nothing as a student reached for the goblin saying, "You're so cute."

It took a blinking second before the student noticed the teeth locked around his wrist. Another before he screamed.

I chose to use this as a teaching moment. "Don't put your hand near sharp objects. Understood?"

Fervent nods.

Since I didn't have a clear headshot, I went hands-on. I jammed my thumbs into the hinges of the goblin's jaws. When it unlocked, I wrapped an arm around its neck and held it while two of my students jumped in to secure its limbs.

Only then did I let go and eye the sobbing student. "Next time, pay attention to the rules. Find a medic." I turned away. We didn't coddle stupidity in Hell.

"Jerod." I waved a hand, and the boy stacked the last goblin into a neat cord with the others. Thirteen. The usual number for a goblin gang.

"What should we do with them?" Jerod nudged a stubby-nosed goblin on the bottom.

"Don't ask me. I need to go home and pack. I hear the kindergarten for Gifted Demonic Children is looking for some new toys."

The bugged-out eyes on the goblins amused my acolytes as they scurried off with the donation. A short-lived amusement that quickly turned weary. It never changed. My life a never-ending saga of goblin catching, text restoration, and acolyte training. The only reprieve from monotony that I ever got was the raising of my nephew when his parents died.

However, his time with me was coming to an end, hence the reason I was taking a vacation. In the morning, we'd be leaving on a goodbye cruise. The nephew I'd raised approached the end of his life in a human body. Soon, a curse upon his line—passed down through generations—would strike, making him into a permanent sea monster.

Which really sucked. I still remembered the day Ian had come into my care, arriving along with news of my much younger sister's demise. A solemn-eyed toddler, he'd gazed at me, doing his best to still a trembling lower lip. My first impulse as a confirmed bachelor was to send him to the orphanage. What did I know about raising a child?

Yet there was something in his face... He reminded me of his mother, but even more, I saw *me*. A mini-me, the son I'd never had.

"Guess we'd better move some books around and make room for you," I'd said.

At the time, my home, the home of a scholar, hosted thousands upon thousands of tomes. Books that over the years found themselves returned to the library as Ian, my nephew and new son, grew. The evacuation made room in my house for a child who educated me more than any book could. He taught me that there was a world outside of my studies. Showed me what it could be like to share my day with someone else. He made me crave the company of others. Reminded me what life had been like before I became a demi-demon in Lucifer's service.

And now, he was leaving me. It made me sad as I packed my things for our last vacation together, including a satchel of books. A proper librarian never left home without at least a half-dozen. Except, I wasn't actually a librarian any more. I'd finally tendered my resignation to the devil's shock. Retirement meant more time to do the things I wanted.

Like this cruise. I made my way to the port where I ran into my nephew, who managed a weak smile.

"Got your ticket?" my nephew Ian asked.

"Yes, I've got my ticket. I'm old, not senile."

"Are you sure? I heard you let goblins loose in the library again."

"Who, me?" My lips curved. "How else am I supposed to train the newbies properly?"

"One of these days, they'll catch on to the fact that you're playing them."

"Who says they haven't? On the contrary, once they realize the emergency is faked, they become part of the story that continues it." In order to teach, I used awe. Reverence of my skills. The acolytes saw me going after goblins, snaring them with ease. They eagerly listened to everything I said after that.

"Yeah, well, they might not mind it, but I'm still pissed you had those brine burrs sink the ship I traveled on when I was ten."

That brought back a fond memory. I'd been trying to teach Ian about accepting his kraken side.

Learning to work with it in the hopes he wouldn't completely lose himself later.

"You survived."

"You could have warned me the burrs on their bodies would stick to the insides of my mouth."

"How was I to know you'd lack common sense and eat them?" Never even occurred to me to tell the kid not to eat something called brine burrs. We figured out it was his monster side making him do that shit. It needed to be taught so he didn't end up a mindless beast like his father.

"Ready for sunshine and cold beverages?" Ian faked enthusiasm as he indicated the portal. Our turn to go through.

"You forgot bikinis."

"Did you bring yours?" Ian taunted before striding towards the inter-dimensional rip.

It rippled on the dock, and nothing could be seen through that hole to somewhere else. We could be stepping into a volcano for all we knew. Yet when I passed into the rip, feeling the pressure and cold of nothing and the sum of everything at once, I exited from the ashy heat of Hell to the moist sunshine of the Caribbean.

It had been a while since I'd tasted the atmosphere of Earth. I'd only been back a few times since I was cursed to become a demi-demon. Tilting my head back, the hot rays of the sun kissed my skin. I breathed deeply, inhaling all kinds of smells that weren't brimstone and ash. Brine, the whiff of smoke from a stack, a bit of ocean decay. Not all that nice, yet it wasn't Hell. "Damn that smells good."

"Incoming!" yelled an imp waving a fluorescent glow stick.

My nephew nudged me, and we moved to allow the next person through. My steps soon slowed as I glanced overhead, noting a pair of incoming witches on brooms. An older woman and a young lady. For a moment, my heart stuttered. I used to know a girl who rode a broom back in the day.

But she got married. Had a child. Once I realized she'd moved on without me, breaking my heart in the process, I'd never looked her up again. Nor did I ever care for another like I did my sweet witch, Dorothy.

"Did someone piss in your coffee? You look so sad. Don't tell me you're going to be a sour-faced downer this entire trip," Ian teased me. He'd been making light of his demise for a while now.

I didn't laugh. I couldn't help but feel I'd let him down.

"I will be a grumpy old demon if I want to," I grumbled.

"Maybe putting on a bathing suit and going for a

dip will soothe your crotchety tendencies." Ian held the elevator door open, waiting for me.

What would I do without him? "You're a mouthy brat."

"Learned from the best."

I hid a smile.

Ian tucked his hands into his pockets and slouched against the elevator wall. "So, I saw you eyeing those witches. You going to try and hook up with someone?"

"I am not here to get laid."

"Why not? I'm thinking I should have a last hurrah." He winked at me, and my heart turned sadder. I saw right through the attempt but played along.

"We should find sisters."

"Don't you mean a mother and daughter pair?" Age-wise, I was much older than my nephew, but in appearance, not quite old enough to be his dad.

The elevator spilled us out onto a floor well above water. Our lavish suites were side by side. A good thing because I wanted to be close to my nephew in his final hours.

We chose to split up and unpack. We'd meet again for dinner. I'd no sooner closed my door than a certain goddess decided to visit me.

Springtime flowers filled the room a moment before she swirled into view.

"Gaia, I thought we discussed knocking."

The pretty goddess of nature, wearing a light green summer frock, a crown of woven daisies, and a chocolate handprint over her boob, inclined her head. "If I appeared in the hallway to knock, then people might remark on the fact that I was visiting you. Not a good idea since we don't want Lucifer finding out I'm sneaking off to see another man and lying to him."

She put it in terms of the worst-case scenario possible. The reminder brought a groan. "I really wish you'd tell your husband what we're doing." Because I didn't need the hassle of dealing with an angry Lord of Hell. He tended to be quite jealous where his wife was concerned.

"You know we can't tell! He would lose his ever suspicious and possessive mind." She stamped her foot, and I was sure they felt the ground quake somewhere in the world.

"We're not doing anything wrong."

"Other than going behind his back."

"Then tell him," I begged.

"Tell him I'm researching a prophecy predicting his demise at the hands of his own child? Are you crazy? We'd be better off telling him we're having an affair."

True. I might survive, especially if I agreed to a threesome. "I am impressed you managed to convince the king of Atlantis to let the cruise visit his city island."

Gaia smirked. "I said 'Tsunami,' and Rexxie said, 'Anything you'd like, Goddess.' It took them centuries to recover from the last time I wiped them out for being disrespectful."

"Here's to hoping we find a copy of the prophecy." Because it was missing from Hell's library. Every mention of it had been wiped out. Yet I knew it existed because I'd seen it once, a long, long time ago. The day a certain witch had come to see me as a matter of fact.

That meeting didn't end well, and the book had gone off for restoration. It never returned. Disappeared, all trace of it gone. I'd been searching for it ever since. Never found the original, but I did run into a rumor. An ancient Mesopotamian god who never left his cave told me to check the library in Atlantis.

Problem was getting there. For centuries, the city had been hidden under the ocean.

"That old story probably has nothing to do with my precious baby," Gaia said, wringing her hands.

"But I have to be sure. Have you seen the petition circulating about Damian's title?"

I had. Someone had started a campaign to have Lucifer's son declared a simple dark prince. They claimed he couldn't be the Antichrist since he had been born in wedlock, a product of loving and willing parents. The followers of the End of Times, who expected one day to be led by the Antichrist, demanded a true Son of Perdition. One achieved during a proper ravishment of a mortal woman during a dark rite involving blood sacrifice.

Lucifer might have agreed if Mother Nature hadn't promised castration if she caught him screwing around on her.

Needless to say, the devil chose to ignore the petition and obey his wife.

"Not all prophecies come to pass," I reminded Gaia.

After all, the one about her daughter predicted she'd also bring about the apocalypse. Instead, Muriel had settled down with a few men—four at last count, although there were wagers a fifth would be coming. Lucifer's daughter even had a kid and was disgustingly suburban—Lucifer's words, not mine. He'd said the fact that she had orgies with her four men was the only reason he'd not disowned her for leading such a normal, happy life.

"I am aware that some prophecies shift over time. Actions have reactions. But something's nagging me about this one." Gaia worried, and the flowers in her crown wilted.

"Is this because of that meme being passed around Snaphell and Hellbook?" It showed the nebulous figure of the Antichrist standing on the bodies of his parents and crushing the Earth in his fist while chuckling darkly.

"Damian would never kill me." I noticed how she didn't include Lucifer in that assertion. Too many predictions said the devil would die by the hand of his son.

"Damian is but a small child with many years ahead of him to decide what kind of man he'll be. One shaped by you and his father."

She groaned. "That's what I'm afraid of. I swear, I don't know how Muriel turned out so good in Lucifer's care."

"Maybe she turned out fine because he's a good dad?" It sounded wrong to even say it.

Gaia's nose wrinkled. "Does a good father threaten to feed his child to the hellhounds if he shits through his nappy one more time?"

"I'm sure he wouldn't." Not my most reassuring statement.

"He'd better not. But I don't need Luc finding any

more excuses to eliminate Damian. Which is why you need to find that prophecy for me. To debunk it before my husband finds it."

"This would have been easier and faster if you'd just snapped your fingers and taken me to Atlantis for a peek," I grumbled.

"I would have, but they installed some kind of dampener since my last visit."

"Can't whirl your way in?"

"No," she said, sounding most disgruntled. "The nerve of that king, spelling Atlantis against me."

"Join me when we dock there in a few days and show them who's boss."

Gaia shook her head. "I am tempted but shouldn't. There is something wrong with that island. A lack of connection to the land, *my land*, weakens me."

I had a theory about that. "It's because Atlantis was built almost entirely from the sea."

She grimaced. "And the ocean depths, including its denizens, belong to the Neptune family. But who helped them build those kelp farms and created those pretty-colored corals? Me. Yet I don't get any credit." Gaia scowled, and somewhere, a tornado probably tore up a few trees.

"Utterly unfair," I agreed.

"I should get going. The baby will wake soon." A

good mother, Gaia didn't leave home for long these days, given Damian proved to be a demanding son of the devil. Like father, like the child of his loins. Gaia spoiled the boy rotten, and thus far, no one had dared interfere. There were, however, wagers on just how bad the little prince would become.

"I can't keep doing these favors for you," I reiterated, not for the first time.

Her smile caused butterflies to burst free from the cascade of her hair and flit around the room in a riot of brightness. "I do so appreciate it. You are the best librarian there is. The one most suited to finding secrets. And keeping them."

Flattery. Even an old demon wasn't immune.

"I am only doing it because I've never seen the Atlantis library." Nobody had since it sank. What kind of wonders did it hold? Ancients secrets. The best kind.

"Be sure to report to me the moment you locate something."

"What if there's nothing to find?"

"I'm sure you'll finagle an interesting tidbit. If you do, I'll grant you a boon."

"Better be a good one." Because if Lucifer found out that I was working with his wife, I'd be feeding the hounds.

"Oh, it's good." Gaia winked. "You'll soon see. Now, I must be off. Have fun."

"Doubtful."

"Ah, yes, the nephew thing." She knew right away the source of my turned-down lips. "I wouldn't worry too much. I have a feeling things will work themselves out."

"Really?" A goddess alluding to the future? Truth, or telling me what I wanted to hear so I wouldn't be distracted from her task? I didn't doubt for one moment that she'd manipulate me if it suited her purposes.

Rather than clarify her statement, Gaia said, "You should get yourself a drink. I hear the piña coladas are especially nice when sipped on the fifth-level deck." With that advice, she swirled out of sight.

I went looking for a cocktail. The day needed some alcohol.

I almost choked on a candied cherry—because the colada came decked out and frothy—when I heard *her* voice. "Hello, Shax. It's been a long time."

2

DOROTHY: A LADY SHOULD ALWAYS BE PLEASANT. EVEN WITH JERKS

I DON'T KNOW what possessed me. I could have avoided Shax. Just walked right on past and he might never have even noticed.

He certainly didn't see me back in the day. I'd tried so hard to get Shax to look at me with smoldering heat instead of friendly interest. But the man was more excited about some arcane tidbit in a dusty book than the fact that I'd worn a new frock.

Shax, the librarian. No last name that I ever heard. Once a person joined that almost religious institution, they shed their past. I had thought for a while they might also discard their sexuality, given Shax never showed any interest.

And I tried. Coy smiles. The fleeting touch of my hand on his. Back then, I'd even been scandalous enough to show him my ankles.

But Shax only had one love—his books.

That scholarly bent saw him shunned by his family, who took more pride in the males who followed a warriors path. Yet the disapproval didn't stop Shax from following his passion.

For knowledge. Not me.

It still burned. Kind of like the library I'd accidentally helped to partially destroy. In my defense, the fire had been accidental and not entirely my fault. The flood, however...

All in the past. Just like my crush on him.

Shax looked at me, his eyes not the deep brown I recalled. A ruddy hue filled the depths, but the same thick lashes framed them. He met my gaze and didn't look away. The shyness of before vanished.

This new directness took me by surprise. I expected him to ask who I was. After all, it had been centuries since we'd seen each other. I'd changed.

So had he. I recognized him, but barely. It was his good looks that had initially caught my attention. A handsome guy, lounging in a chair, his features matured into a craggy ruggedness with a tan that belied his scholarly pursuits. His thick, dark hair had hints of silver at the temples. His horns, part of the deal that'd turned him demi-demon were trimmed short.

It reminded me of an expression. *The bigger the*

horns, the tinier the brains. It might be why the devil didn't have any. Lucifer might play the part of dumb rube, but that façade only hid the sharpest mind.

"Dottie."

Hearing the old nickname did something to my heart. Shax remembered me.

I did my best to not stutter. A woman of my years had grace and confidence. A mere male could not frazzle me. I gave him my coldest regard. "It's been a while." Since the day I'd thrown caution to the wind and kissed him. It'd turned into a fire, a real one that'd resulted in him throwing me out of the library. And his life.

At least I had the fortitude not to go back, begging for forgiveness.

"You look…" He eyed me, and while he masked any revulsion, I had to wonder what he thought. I knew perfectly well how I appeared. Old. After all, on the human plane, I was a grandmother, a talented witch living as a woman in my sixties. "…really good."

"And you've gotten better at lying."

A slow smile crossed his lips. "Would I lie to an old friend?"

"I don't know."

"It's been a while."

"Has it?" I played dumb, mostly because I remembered exactly how long it'd been. Too long. Back when I was a simple witch in training.

"Are you going on this cruise?"

My lips twitched. "Evidence would say yes given we've left shore." Which meant we were both stuck on board. Didn't bother me one bit. Especially since I could leave the ship anytime I wanted. Portals could be opened and, if close enough to land, I could hop a broom and sweep myself to shore.

Run away, though? No. I could totally handle Shax. He meant nothing to me.

And I meant nothing to him. He appeared calm and collected. Suave even.

"How you been?" He injected a bit of Joey in there. If you'd never heard that character from the sitcom *Friends,* that basically meant Shax talked smoothly and sexily. It proved jarring, as did the deeper voice.

In the years long past, he used to stammer and never meet my gaze. At the time, I adored that about him, even as it frustrated me.

"I've been quite excellent. You?" I kept smiling even as I wanted to leave. Why torture myself talking to him? And me at such a disadvantage. He looked good, and I was old.

Shax didn't immediately reply. He stared at me. Intently.

I said nothing. Just waited.

"As a matter of fact, it hasn't been all that great."

"Didn't make it past librarian's assistant?" I sneered. Okay, so I wasn't past being petty.

"Actually, I am head librarian now. Everyone works for me."

"Congratulations." Not completely insincere. If he'd attained the post, then he'd obviously worked hard to get it.

"No one ever explained that being the boss came with so many annoyances, though. I can see why Lucifer hates his job."

"Close to the devil these days, are you?"

"Ever since we made the deal for these." He waved to his horns.

"What happened to not selling your soul? You were so against it." I still remembered him telling me that he'd never agree to a deal with Lucifer. One I'd helped broker with the dark lord.

He stared at me as I told him my news. "The Lord of Hell says he can save your library from the coming cataclysm. But it has to be soon." Everyone was evacuating before the lava could take out the entire city.

"There's a price," Shax said. He didn't look me in the eyes as he spoke. He rarely did. "To save the library, I must let the devil transform me."

"Into a demi-demon?" The closest he could get to remaining human. "There are so many advantages."

"Are you here to promote the positive points?" He spoke more harshly than I'd ever heard. "I'll live longer. Be stronger."

He made it sound bad. "You will be able to protect the library. Isn't that what you want?" Whereas I had selfish reasons for wanting him to make the deal. As a powerful sea witch with a deal already in place with Lucifer, I'd be long-lived. As a human, Shax wouldn't be.

"It requires that I relinquish my soul to him."

"It's not as bad as it sounds. I've already promised my soul to the devil," I reminded.

"I want to be me," Shax replied. "Not a demon."

"Not all demons are bad."

"But they aren't human."

"Neither am I."

His reply snapped me back to the present. "It occurred to me in those last days that I could either save the library and myself or lose it all. I chose to live."

"And now you regret it. Typical." I snorted.

"Actually, being a demi-demon isn't bad. It has allowed me to achieve every single goal I set for myself. What I didn't realize was how hollow those would feel."

"You should count yourself lucky. Lucifer rarely

changes humans anymore." The dark lord had never said *why* he stopped doing it, but I figured it had to do with giving part of himself to effectuate the change. The demons Lucifer created were stronger than those born.

"At least being a demi-demon is better than living the life of the unliving as a ghoul or vampire. I don't know if I could handle being trapped on Earth with an allergy to sunlight."

"Vampires are now considered sexy."

"You trying to tell me I chose wrong?" He grinned at me.

"You fishing for a compliment?"

He winked.

Shax *winked*.

Hell must have frozen over again.

"So, you like being a demi-demon and get to be the library's big boss. Still not seeing how your life sucks."

"Perhaps sucks isn't the right word. Empty maybe. Lonely."

"You should get a dog."

"Not that kind of lonely."

"There are dating services these days you can use. And last I heard, you can still rent by the hour."

His lips curved. "I see you're sharper than ever. I always liked that about you."

He did?

"Don't let the body fool you. It's only a wrapper." Inside, I was still in my prime.

"I imagine you can shed it at will, like a chrysalis. It would be interesting to see what shape you took."

"Still would be the same on the inside."

"Sugar and spice, naughty and nice." The grin he offered held a hint of the devil. Perhaps influence of his maker.

He had aptly summed me up, though. I might be a witch, but I wasn't pure evil. Just like the devil wasn't all torture and angst. Some kind of balance had to exist. Too far one way, and you got the despots who were kept chained in Hell. Too far the other, and you had those pompous angels with their noses in the air who wouldn't lift a hand to do anything.

"And how would you describe yourself?" I asked.

"Complex."

I snorted. "Give me a break. If that's supposed to make you sound mysterious, then it failed."

"So, you think you know me?"

"You can't have changed that much." I said it, and yet the proof stood before me. He'd changed. A lot!

"Did you come on the cruise alone?"

"If you're fishing to know if I'm single, then yes, I am." No point in lying. He had connections and could check. "But not interested in dating. Especially not you." I meant to fluster him.

Instead, he gave me the cockiest grin. "I accept the challenge."

My mouth rounded into an O of surprise, mostly because the Shax I remembered never volunteered to do anything. He took orders.

"This is not some kind of game. I really am not interested in dating you."

"Because you feel like you don't know me. Totally understandable. We'll rectify that."

"Please. You are not going to date me looking like this."

He eyed me most seriously. "Why not? Are you claiming that I can only be interested in superficial cosmetics and not the person themselves?"

"Do not turn this around. You cannot seriously tell me you're attracted." I'd not aged well. I couldn't have said why. I chose to let myself turn into a caricature of what I thought a grandma should be.

"Really, Dottie. Where are your morals? Already talking about sex when we've barely just met."

I almost knocked the mocking smirk from his face. "There will be no sex." Hotly declared even though my old body actually had some interest.

"If you say so."

"I do say so."

"We can discuss it more later. I have dinner plans, but I don't think we've got anything happening after."

"You're not here alone?" Sudden hot jealousy filled me.

"No."

My heart might have shrunk a little at the words. "Cad!"

His lips quirked. "I'm here with my nephew."

The jealousy subsided. "You have a nephew?"

"A pair of them, actually. A few times removed in one case, but they're family. Ian actually came to live with me. This is a bon voyage trip for us."

"He's moving out? Can you give me tips to give my granddaughter?" Jane had been living with me since her parents died. Now thirty, it was time she moved on. Heck, *I* needed to move on.

"Not exactly moving out. It's complicated."

I rolled my eyes. "So I'm beginning to understand."

"You should meet him. Ian's a good kid. A shame about the curse on his line."

I wouldn't ask. I wouldn't ask. I… "What kind of curse?"

His lips stretched, and his eyes gave off a reddish glow. "If he doesn't find a true mate in someone from a particular bloodline before his thirty-second birthday, then life as he knows it will end."

"Tough curse."

"No kidding, especially since we can't find someone in that family that might be suitable."

I didn't need to ask to know that the birthday would be soon. "What happens at thirty-two? Does he die?"

"He becomes a kraken. Permanently."

"I'm sorry." I truly was. I understood how curses could suck. My own daughter had been caught by one because of her pirate husband. He'd made a deal that gave him a longer, tougher life in order to be with my witch daughter. But when it came due, they'd both died, and now lived as part of the ocean, tied to it until someone else took over. That deadline was why, after eons of being together, they'd had a child. Jane. At least something of them lived on.

"I didn't know his dad well, so when it happened, I didn't pay it much mind." Shax shrugged. "But with Ian, it's different."

"You raised him." A nice thing to do. I didn't let it soften my stance towards him.

"Best thing to ever happen to me. But problem is, now I care for the kid, and I can't stop the curse."

"Surely, you found something in your library." He was the head of it.

"We only recently discovered the terms of the curse. Damned bureaucracy. Lost for centuries, it turned up less than two weeks ago."

"And you're out of time," I said softly. "That's why you want me to meet him." A curse was comprised of magic. I could play with magic.

"I know you might not be able to do anything."

Curses, much like elastic bands, had a tendency to snap and cause some pain.

"Doesn't hurt to look. Bring him by to see me." Only after I offered did I realize I needed to give him a room number. "On second thought, I'll come find you."

"How about dinner?"

"I thought you were busy." I arched a brow. Funny how acting coy had no age.

"I am. With Ian. It's the perfect time for you to meet him."

"According to you," I muttered. "Will it only be your nephew, or will there be any other family members? Maybe your own kids?" Yeah, I dug...not so subtly.

"Never had any. You?"

"Just the daughter. And now a granddaughter." The reminder that a lifetime of experiences existed between us.

"Lucky. That is my one regret. I never had my own family."

"Why not?"

His jaw tensed, and for a moment, he was the boy I remembered who ducked his head. "Never found the time. Probably the biggest mistake I made. Not paying attention to the world passing me by. Losing out on opportunities."

At those words, his gaze met mine, the expression intent.

Captivating.

It took an effort to look away. "Nice seeing you. I should go now."

"Say you'll come to dinner."

My heart skipped. Back in the day, I was the one asking him to have a meal with me. Making him supper, toiling over it all day in that hot kitchen only to have him show up late because he'd gotten caught up in a book. Or, at the end of our friendship, not showing up at all as he sought a way to save the library.

"I'm busy." This wasn't entirely a pleasure cruise. I'd come along to watch over my granddaughter. The love spell I'd cast on her locket was behaving oddly.

"You're lying."

"It's called being polite instead of telling you I

have no interest in spending time with you." My anger at him was slightly irrational. The only wrong he'd done to me was not returning my affection. And now, after centuries had passed, he wanted to flirt?

I hated that it worked. Seeing Shax again reminded me of all the things he used to make me feel. The tingles. The breathlessness.

I wasn't a young girl of inexperience anymore. I should have better control of myself.

"Not interested? No." He shook his head. "You're lying again?" The words held a hint of uncertainty.

"Why are you pushing me?" I felt trapped even as he didn't do anything overt.

"Because I want to see you. Hear what's happened to you. Spend time with you."

I blinked at his obstinance. "Well, too bad."

"I will keep asking until you say yes."

"And I will keep saying no! Jerk!"

A woman stopped beside me. "Grandma, please don't tell me you're harassing this gentleman."

I could have cringed as Jane called me Grandma. Grandmas were old. I didn't feel old.

"I am not harassing Shax," I huffed. "Merely indicating that I'm unavailable for meals since we are traveling together."

Jane arched a brow. "Since when are you hooking up with me for food? You told me, and I repeat, 'I love you Janey Waney, but you need to make some friends and loosen up. Because I will be, and I can't have you cramping my style.'"

"That's something a whore would say." I lifted my nose and sniffed in disdain. I was quite sure I'd put it more politely when I talked to Jane. But perhaps not. After all, she needed to hang with someone closer to her age who wasn't related to her.

Jane eyed Shax. "Your name…" She tapped her lip. "Sounds familiar."

"Nope. Not one bit. Let's go check out shuffle head." I linked my arm with Jane's and dragged her away before Shax could say anything.

Not that he could say much. We'd never actually dated. The only time I'd kissed him, it'd started a fire.

Walking away didn't stop Jane from bugging me. "He's cute. You going to have dinner with him?"

"Most certainly not."

"Just going to skip right to the drinks and his bed. Efficient. I like it."

I coughed. A bit too hard. She pounded me on the back. When I could gasp for air, I said, "I can't believe you just said that to me."

"Me either." She scrunched her nose. "There's something in the air, I swear. It's making me a little crazy."

"You'll be fine. Why not go find a drink. Get some food."

"Nope. I'm not getting drunk. I'm going to hang out in the room. Catch up on some reading."

"Great plan." I shoved at her, not arguing with her choice. The love spell locket was aboard the ship, the magic already at work. My granddaughter wouldn't have a choice. She'd leave her room because her true mate was somewhere on this ship.

With her out of the way, and Shax nowhere in sight, I could finally answer a summons.

I found the tiki bar on a lower level. Tucked away, it only had a few people inside. One of them being the devil.

He wore a wide-brimmed straw hat, big sunglasses, a shirt peppered in neon sloths, and flip-flops that showed his six-toed feet. "Took you long enough," he grumbled, gesturing to the many platters of food, most half-eaten.

I slid into the seat across from Lucifer. "I can't drop everything just because you call. Stop whining like a little girl and tell me you ordered something with lots of alcohol for me." Never show weakness with the devil.

"I drank it." He lifted his hand and waggled four fingers. "We'll get more."

"What are you doing here? Does Gaia know

you've left?" My understanding was that the devil had agreed to co-parent the newest dark prince. And by co-parent, that meant fifty-fifty with a pair of gods used to doing whatever they liked.

"The spawn of my loins is being watched by someone trustworthy."

"Don't say Nefertiti."

"How did you guess?" He beamed.

"I can't believe you. You know she's a bad influence." I shook my head.

"Exactly. Can you think of anyone better to corrupt my son? Other than me, of course." He grinned, layers of sharp teeth showing, and yet he still managed to look disturbingly human. Handsome, too.

Still, despite his good looks and evil nature, he didn't give me tingles like a certain other old demon.

"I'm supposed to be on vacation. Why are you here?" I asked.

"Can't a dark lord visit his favorite witch?"

I arched a brow. "Since when am I the favorite? Last I heard, isn't that Ysabel's title?" Everyone knew the devil had a thing for his secretary. Problem being she only had a thing for her husband, Remy.

"She is no fun since the child. Brings it to work and everything. Can you believe she instituted workplace rules about watching while she feeds it on the tit? Never wears a skirt anymore. I've been forbidden —me, the devil—forbidden from ass-slapping the staff. Male or female. My jokes aren't being laughed at anymore. The HR department is involved in numerous lawsuits about sexual harassment. It's unfair! I'm the devil. It's an insult if I don't say something about your breasts or cop an inappropriate feel."

"You haven't done either with me. And I'm not insulted."

"You should be. It's because I don't find you appealing. Why do you persist in adopting such a shell?" He waved his hand.

"The same reason you looked twenty years older for such a long time. It suits the purpose."

"You should try shedding this body for a new one. It can revive even the most jaded." He winked. "And you can go for hours. Days."

I didn't reply because the devil would just keep going, each thing he said getting dirtier and dirtier. Two could play at that game. "Rumor has it you love your wife so much you won't cheat on her."

Lucifer eyed me, and smoke began to curl from his ears. "Are you accusing me of chivalry?"

"Actually, I was accusing you of monogamy."

"Even worse!" he roared. The tiki bar trembled.

The mural of a monkey god suddenly possessed glowing eyes, and its mouth moved.

"Oh, calm down. If it upsets you that much, you big baby, then start slapping asses again and asking women to come home with you."

"I can't. The lawyers, you know? My hands are tied."

"Sure, they are." It amused me to see him fighting to never publicly admit his affection for Gaia, and yet it was quite clear for anyone to see.

"Lawsuits aside, we should discuss why I'm here. I need you to do me a favor."

"Depends." Because one learned early on not to agree without knowing the details first. "What's the favor?"

"I need you to find out what my head librarian Shax is up to."

My mouth went dry. "Why? What do you think he's guilty of?"

Lucifer jabbed a shrimp in my direction. "I initially thought he was boinking my wife, then I realized how ridiculous it was that she'd choose his less-than-impressive self over me."

"Naturally."

"So, I wondered, what is she up to that requires her being alone with another man and has her returning looking furtive? Why is it that the other day, she returned sopping wet, smelling of fish, and fuming? It apparently wasn't because she didn't properly shower. Quite insulted she was too, for some reason."

"Get to the point," I grumbled.

"It's a long point, so pay attention. Isn't it a huge coincidence that Atlantis, which has just resurfaced for the first time in centuries, is a destination for a brand-new cruise? One my wife has an itinerary for on her Hell phone."

"How would you know?"

"Do you really think I don't stalk my wife?" Lucifer rolled his eyes.

"If you're such a good stalker, why do you need me?"

Lucifer scowled. "Because Gaia is wily. She keeps evading me, but I know she's been on this ship. And do who you know who else is on this ship? My head librarian. The one she's been visiting for the last few weeks. He's suddenly taking a vacation. Strange. Hence why I procured you some excellent accommodations."

Which meant in the bowels of the ship, in a tiny closet of a room that I shared with Jane. Noisy as all hell, too. Brilliant on the devil's part as he ensured I'd spend little time in it and would eagerly do his bidding.

"You think Shax is conspiring against you with your wife?"

"Yes. And I believe whatever it is has to do with Atlantis."

"Could be he's interested in a cure for his nephew."

"Why would he want to get rid of the curse? Killian will be the mightiest of sea beasts. A lord of the ocean. Why, he could even annoy the piss out of Neptune if he chose. That's not a curse. It's a bloody miracle."

I shook my head, mostly in admiration. "You are a true demon at heart."

"Some days it's good to be evil. Which is to say, it's good to be me." The dark lord had a grin that would terrify even a killer clown.

Glad he was happy. I, on the other hand, found myself quite annoyed. Especially since I knew exactly what Lucifer attempted with his appearance. "You are trying to set me up," I huffed.

Not the first time the devil played matchmaker. I'd avoided previous attempts quite easily. Somehow, he must have gotten wind of my long-ago crush on Shax. Then fabricated a reason for us to be on a cruise together, and now, threw me at my ex-crush in the hopes of pairing us up.

It wouldn't happen. Lucifer might have managed

some impossible hookups in the past, but Shax and I would never be a couple.

"Me? Try to put together a fabulous old witch and a just-as-old demon? Never." The rebuttal was way too overblown.

"Why would you even bother? We're too old to be making babies." In this body, at any rate. I eyed it. There were spells I could use...

"Can't a dark lord just want to see two of his loyal minions find their happily ever after?"

"No." With Lucifer, there was always an angle.

"Are your feelings going to be a problem?" He went from joking to serious, badass Lord of Hell. "I gave you an order. Find out what Shax is doing. Make sure he's not doing my wife."

"And if he is?"

The devil smiled. "Then I hope you're not too attached."

3

SHAX: I REALLY WISH SOMEONE COULD RECOMMEND A BOOK THAT EXPLAINS WOMEN.

I DIDN'T KNOW what I'd done to piss Dottie off, and yet there was no denying she was angry. Odd, since she had been the one to abruptly sever our friendship when she left without a word. I'd found out what'd happened later via rumor.

She appeared old now, on the waning edge of life. I had to wonder why she chose to age. A witch of her abilities surely knew how to combat it. After all, she had some demon blood in her line. However, she appeared matronly, her hair a whitish gray cap of fuzz, her clothing the pastel monstrosities often seen in retirement communities—comfort being key. Her skin was wrinkled as if she didn't know of any creams to moisturize.

Why had she let herself go?

Only one answer came to mind.

She must still mourn the loss of her husband.

When I found out that she'd married, and in turn stopped visiting the library, I assumed she'd found her grand love. I'd also gone on a bender that involved waking up a few weeks later with a tattoo on my ass and no recollection of anything but a healthy respect from the tavern regulars I'd apparently gotten maudlin with.

I put Dottie out of my mind and not long after made the deal to become a demi-demon. I saved my library. Disappeared into Hell and threw myself into my work. I spent centuries not really feeling anything, and only truly woke up again at Ian's arrival on my doorstep.

Seeing Dottie, though... I could feel a quickening in my blood. A perk of interest.

Call me pathetic, but I still harbored feelings for her.

I remembered all too well the shy smiles we shared back before either of us had truly experienced life. How I'd stuttered around her, my ability to use simple grammar stunted the moment I caught even a hint of her presence. I knew what she was. A witch. Her mother had warned me away, told me it was for my own good. Dorothy was meant for great things, and she would live a long, long time. Whereas I—only a scholar, not a fighter, and human to boot—wasn't a proper match for her. That didn't occur until I became a demi-demon, but by then, it was too late.

Dottie had moved on.

"Fuck me with a giant dildo, could you look more depressed on a cruise through paradise? What the fuck is wrong with you?" The devil stood blocking my view with his obnoxiously bright ensemble.

"Sailor suits went out of style," I remarked.

"I am bringing them back, baby." Lucifer swung his hips and winked.

"What do you want?" I snapped.

"Now, Shax, is that any way to greet your lord and master?" Lucifer pretended to be aggrieved.

I merely scowled. Having served out my contract in Hell, the devil no longer had true reign over me. "I retired from your service."

"Ruining my perfect record, I know. People are supposed to die on the job, literally working them-selves to death. But you...you are actually collecting your pension as of this morning."

"I hardly call getting a piece of coal each week a pension."

"Back in the day, when the bargain was made, it was worth a fortune."

"Why are you here? Don't you have to go feed the baby or something?" I didn't need the devil breathing down my neck, not with me secretly working for his wife.

"I let Nef borrow the little ankle biter." Lucifer angled his leg. "Little fucker clamped on this morning and wouldn't let go. Had to shake like a bunny on ED pills to get him off. Thought Gaia was gonna tear off my head when she caught him. Can you believe she said my yelling 'touchdown' was inappropriate?"

"I can't imagine." Because that seemed like a perfect time to use that expression. "And Gaia's okay with Nefertiti watching the child?"

"Why wouldn't she be? I used to let Muri visit with her all the time. And Bambi credits her time in the tower as the reason she won Slut of the Year so many times in a row. But only because I don't partic-ipate anymore." Lucifer had been the undisputed champ for a long time.

"Hey, if you aren't attached to your head, then who am I to dispute your choice in childcare?" I shrugged.

"I smell the censure in your tone." The devil puffed up his chest.

Such preening had long ago lost its ability to impress. Don't get me wrong, in a knock-them-down battle, Lucifer would hand me my ass. But that didn't mean I rolled over to him.

"Gee, why would anyone have a problem with a sorceress, almost as old as you, caring for an innocent child?"

"Ain't nothing innocent about my son," Lucifer bragged. "And how come you're not bugging Adexios? He has a sea monster watching after his kids."

"Sweets would pulverize anyone who harmed a hair on their heads."

"I know, and it's so unfair. How come I don't have a sea monster?" Lucifer pouting was a scary thing. "Not yet, at any rate. How is Ian doing?" His teeth gleamed.

I glared. "Ian isn't working for you." The devil kept offering, though. Wanted a kraken of his very own on the payroll.

"Then you better help me out."

"With what?" I'd agree to many things to get the devil to walk away from the kid. Yes, kid. At thirty-two, Ian hadn't experienced anything. A child still in so many ways.

"Something weird is going on. I can feel it. Coming from this very ship!" His brows beetled—impressively I might add—actually shifting across his face.

"And what do you expect me to do about it?"

"I need you to be my eyes and ears, Shax. Flush out the threat."

"Other than food poisoning, I highly doubt there's anything on this ship that can hurt you. Or Hell for that matter."

"You can't know that for sure. You haven't even looked."

"I can be sure because even if there was something hinky on board, I'd say it's the humans on this Earth plane that need to worry. Not you. Unless you're planning to bring back the threat if it turns out to be alive."

Lucifer rubbed his chin. "Depends on if it would make a good pet. I'd like to get Damian something unique."

"Why not another dragon? Like you got your granddaughter, Lucinda."

The devil shook his head. "Too simple. I want something a little cooler."

"I swear, you try to give my nephew to your kid as a pet, and we will have a problem."

"Threatening me?" Lucifer huffed some smoke.

"Don't touch Ian."

"You want to make a deal, then you will do my bidding even if you are retired. Must be nice. I'd like to retire, too, you know."

"Then do it."

The devil snorted. "And who would rule Hell in

47

my stead? Remember those times when I stepped down for a little bit?"

Hell had turned into a veritable Hell. Most days, it wasn't bad living there. A bit ashy. Always kind of warm. But in many respects, it was like living on Earth, just more violent and crowded. The human souls didn't always recycle themselves all that quickly. In some ways, the Lilith incident helped. An old, old witch—older even than Lucifer—used souls to power spells. It had cleared out thousands, making room for the ever-incoming influx.

"Okay, so you're needed. Boo. Hoo. You've been doing it for thousands of years. Big deal. Delegate."

"I *have* been delegating," Lucifer grumbled. "And yet, some things require my attention. Did you know my seers are all claiming a calamity is about to strike? Again. And once more, the useless fuckers can't tell me when or what is coming. Dooming me to fail. How hard would it be to tell if it's another flood, meaning I should put in an order for more beach and sailing gear? What if it's an ice age? Totally different wardrobe required. I have an appearance to maintain."

"I know."

The devil had a few halls in the library dedicated to fashion magazines of him. Only one copy per issue. All stored. Every so often, a punishment for a soul involved cataloguing all the various styles.

"We better not be in line for another catastrophic event. It took forever to recover from the deaths last time. And there's more of them now. Imagine, billions of souls coming to my gates, demanding entrance. The paperwork. The crowding. Why, it would be pure...Hell."

The devil hated bureaucracy and yet had his government buried in layers of it. The problem with having too many lawyers and politicians in Hell? Their evil ways rubbed off.

"I'll keep an eye open, but my first priority is still Ian. I am not going to abandon him during his final days."

"Bunch of drama llamas." The devil smirked. "You act as if he's dying."

"He's going to become a kraken forever."

"And? Seems like the perfect life to me. Swim all day. Eat when you want. Mermaids to cater to your every whim. The strength to smash ships and drown sailors." He rubbed his hands in glee.

"Not everyone aspires to be a monster.

"Underachievers."

"Which reminds me, I hear your son is thriving."

At the statement, Lucifer grimaced. "The hellion of my loins is growing. And loud. He yells and expects everyone to drop what they're doing to attend him."

"Meaning he takes after you."

The insult brought a smile to the devil's face. "Chip off the old demon. Which could be a problem. Have you seen the meme circulating around Hell media?"

"Can't say as I have," I lied. Making Lucifer proud I'm sure even as he probably wondered why.

"Some ridiculous cartoon showing Damian killing his mum. And me. But that's to be expected. Not so crazy about the threat to Gaia. I won't have her hurt." Then as if realizing what he admitted, he added gruffly, "If she dies, so does the planet. Can't have that now, can we?"

"No, that would be grave news. But surely the cartoon is just that—satire."

Lucifer looked grave. "I wish it were only that. It was drawn by the great-grandson of Nostradamus."

Hmm. That made it a little more serious. "What will you do about it?"

The Lord of Hell shrugged. "What can I do? If I kill the lad, his mother kills me. Keep him alive, the boy might take my throne."

"Or you could retire and let him take over." I offered a third choice.

Lucifer almost looked sad as he said, "They never

select that option." He shook his head and as if to compensate for being somber, grinned almost maniacally. "Keep your eyes peeled, your dick washed, and be ready to inspect bikinis at any kind of notice. Don't do anything I wouldn't, which is to say, break every law and conduct every sin you can."

"I'll do my best."

"And do let me know if you come across anything that might cause harm to my wife. Could be there is a person with a misguided notion that I need protection from a certain old fable that might be hidden in an old library."

I didn't dare swallow as the devil showed me the astute brain behind the façade.

"I will most certainly inform you of any threat to your family or yourself."

"Do so. And *before* you inform anyone else." Lucifer winked. "It will be our little secret."

He disappeared, and I groaned.

I'm going to be fed to the hounds for sure.

Dinnertime arrived, and I was ready. I knocked on my nephew's cabin door. He answered, already looking half-cut. The drinks came free with our ticket. It seemed Ian was taking advantage.

"Uncle Shax, you are looking spiffy."

"Thanks." I'd dressed to impress in the off-chance Dottie actually showed.

Arriving at the dining level, we took over a table for four people. I and my nephew, but no Dottie. Sure, she'd said no. However, I had a feeling she might show. Or was that false hope?

Ian noticed me scanning the crowd as he nursed a glass of wine, his entrée salad already devoured. At least he was still eating. The boy tasted everything in sight, cramming in every experience he could find.

"Who are you looking for?" he asked.

"Just an old friend. I ran into her earlier."

Ian arched a brow. "An old friend? I thought they were all dead. Or working at the library."

"I have friends outside work," I grumbled.

"Name one."

I frowned. Lucifer or Gaia. No others came to mind, and I wasn't about to use Dottie as an example. "None of your business."

"Man or woman?" he asked, pouring some more wine.

"Woman." No point hiding it. What if she appeared?

"Oooh. Not even a day out of port, and already hooking up," Ian crooned.

"We are not hooking up. Just two old friends, looking to catch up."

"Only old friends? Goodness, and here I thought we used to be more." Her voice hit me first, and I craned my head backwards to see her still looking old.

"Dottie. You made it." I scrambled from my seat and did the courtly thing, pulling out a chair for her. She sat, tucking a giant pleather handbag beside her.

Ian blinked. "This is your Dottie?"

In a moment of drunken weakness, I'd once admitted to my nephew that I loved a girl. "It is. Say hello to Dorothy Pike, the most beautiful girl in the world."

Her lips pursed. "Not a girl. And not so beautiful anymore."

I leaned down as I tucked in her chair. "When I look at you, I still see you in that light blue frock you used to wear, and that sweet smile."

She shivered. I noticed.

Ian also saw and turned pale. "I've heard great things about you."

"Your uncle says you have a problem." Dorothy bluntly put it out there.

"You might say that." Ian's smile was faint.

"I have experience with curses, but I won't promise anything. Give me your hand." She held out hers.

Ian shook his head. "Probably better I don't. I know curses can cause some backlash."

The dumb twat was being a gentleman. I'd taught him well. Too well.

He almost got a cuff as I growled, "Don't be stupid. Give Dottie your hand. She's just going to look."

"I promise you won't hurt me." Dottie winked, looking benign. But I knew better. Even in the library, I'd heard stories of Dorothy. Some called her Tempest due to her witchy powers over the sea.

"Fine." Ian held out his hand.

A fit of strange jealousy consumed me as Dorothy grabbed his palm. I bit down on my inner lip and watched her expression. Once upon a time, she'd worn everything on her face, and I'd been too naïve to read it.

Now, older and wiser, I didn't plan to make the same mistakes.

"The curse is culminating," she remarked, her voice low and monotone. "It's so strong right now in his blood. Almost boiling over. He never bled any of it off to a child."

"No kids," Ian snapped. "This curse dies with me."

"It's intricately wound around him. It's not a simple peel to remove." She let go of his hand and glanced at me. "I'm sorry, but unless he concludes the terms of his curse, I don't think there's anything anyone can do. Whoever laid the spell did it well."

A grimace pulled Ian's face. "Thanks for the honesty. Now, if you don't mind, I think I'm going to get drunk and see how much of my fortune I can gamble away."

I reached for him, and to my surprise, he came in close enough for a hug—and to whisper advice. "Enjoy dinner with your Dottie. I'll see you at breakfast."

I realized then that Ian had created an excuse to leave us alone. I didn't know whether to hug him closer or slap him for playing matchmaker.

Ian left, and Dorothy almost followed.

"Where are you going?" I asked as I sat down, causing her to pause.

"I looked at your nephew as requested."

"But you haven't had dinner." The plate of prime roast landed in front of us, steaming, rare red, and delicious-looking.

"I guess, I could eat." She joined me and proceeded to pack away her meal, then dessert, not saying much. But then again, neither did I.

I instead took in the changes in her, from the plumpness of her cheeks showing an enjoyment of food that she displayed with every savored bite. The curly hair, barely brushed, the streaked gray similar to that of a cloudy day. The lines on her face showed she'd lived a full life with happiness yet sorrow. Smiles and a few scowls.

"You're staring," she grumbled.

"Is that a problem?"

"Yes." She stabbed at a cherry that rolled on her plate.

"You led a full life," I stated.

"Is that a nice way of saying I look ridden hard and put away worn-out?"

"What? No." I chuckled. "More that you had a life. A good one?"

"Yes."

"Until your husband died."

Her lips twitched. "More so after he did. Don't get me wrong. Gerard was a good husband. But a human one. He couldn't understand me."

"I didn't either at the time."

"And you think you do now?" Dottie asked, quirking a brow.

The move was so familiar, I laughed. "No. I would never dare to presume. I'd say you're even more complicated now."

"At least you recognize it."

I sobered. "I always did. You—" I would have said something probably super revealing and sappy, but suddenly, our table wobbled. I glanced at it. Then around me, where nothing else shook.

"Was that you?" she asked.

"No."

The tablecloth began to slide, the cutlery and dishes crashing to the floor. Dottie frowned and used magic to yank it back into place. "We must have tilted."

No, we hadn't. "Give me a second."

I leaned down and shoved my head under the cloth for a peek. A green face peeked out from under the table. Grinned. Turned to look over his shoulder at Dottie's feet. Sensible white runners on them. The creature held up a marker.

"Don't you dare." I dove under the table, hearing Dottie exclaim, "What are you doing?"

I wrestled with the goblin, thumping it between the legs, managing to wrench the marker away from it. The goblin harrumphed and managed to wiggle free but not before jostling the hand with the marker.

The tablecloth lifted, and Dottie glared at me. "Excuse me."

"I know this looks bad," I said from between her legs, the marker in my hand, the tip still pressed against her feminine parts. "There was a goblin."

"On a cruise line of this caliber? On a maiden voyage?" She sniffed.

"I swear. There was a goblin."

"And you're telling me you know how to handle goblins now on top of being head librarian? What's next? Arachnid wrangler? If you're going to pretend, Shax, at least make it believable."

Dottie left, and I spent a moment on the floor gaping. She really didn't have the slightest clue about me. Which made me determined to show her what I was about.

First, I checked on Ian. He was gambling, with a woman on his lap. Good for him! He deserved every ounce of pleasure he could wring with the time he had left.

Then I went looking for a drink and ended up finding Dottie in the lounge. I deliberately sat beside her.

She delivered a side-eye. "You again. Don't see a fellow in centuries, and suddenly he's crowding me."

"Just rekindling a friendship."

"Were we ever friends, Shax?" She gave me a challenging stare. "Because I recall you telling me to get out of your face after a tiny little booboo."

"You destroyed several hundred irreplaceable works."

"By accident. Technically, you started that fire when you knocked over the candle."

"Because you snuck up on me." Intent on my work, I hadn't expected her voice to distract me.

And I most certainly hadn't been prepared for her kiss.

"The candle was your fault," she insisted.

"Agreed. But the water you drenched that section of the library in to put it out?" I reminded.

Her lips quirked. "Overkill."

"Just by about ten thousand tons."

"I'll admit I miscalculated the magic. You didn't have to throw me out of your life."

I gaped at her. Perhaps a little dumbly. "When did I tell you to get out of my life?"

"You told me to leave."

I remembered the incident as if it had happened yesterday.

I was working on a particularly interesting book written in an ancient language no one remained to teach. I'd been muddling along, trying to figure it out, when Dottie marched into the section of the library I'd staked out as my own. I'd spread all my things out on a table and was bent over when she arrived.

My head remained bowed, my interest in the book feigned lest she guess how attuned I was to her presence. I sensed more than saw her moving close behind me.

When she placed her hands over my eyes, she whispered, "Surprise."

"What are you doing here?" I asked, my heart racing so fast and pounding so hard, I feared she'd hear it. I

never understood why she came to see me. Why she always smiled.

She smiled at me now as she said, "Looking for you. I haven't seen you around. I missed you." Then she did the most astonishing thing. She leaned in and kissed me.

On the lips.

It startled me enough that I jumped. My elbow knocked into a candle. It toppled right onto my book.

"Uh-oh."

The dry pages immediately ignited and, infused with panic, I slapped at the flames.

"Hold on, I can put it out." Dorothy snapped her fingers before I could warn her. Back in the day, the library didn't have protection against magic.

I felt the power of it a moment before the space flooded. And I mean flooded. *A tidal wave appeared out of nowhere and soaked not just the book on fire, but me, and that entire section of the library.*

It lasted only a few astonished blinks, then the water receded, leaving a few fish high and dry. Everything else in the section dripped. Utterly soaked, including an astonished Dorothy, who wasn't supposed to be there.

Who'd used witch powers.

The realization horrified. Not the fact that she could do such a thing, but that others would soon know if they found her. Would know and want to harm her. I couldn't allow that to happen.

"I think you should go."

"I—" She looked devastated. *I wished I had time to tell her I would handle this. Keep her safe from the consequences. But I couldn't do that if she didn't leave.*

"Go. Now. Before anyone sees you."

Only in retrospect did I see how perhaps she might have misconstrued my words.

"You thought I wanted you permanently gone?" I snorted, then chuckled, then grew quiet as I suddenly realized what that misconception meant. "I told you to leave so you wouldn't be around when the other librarians arrived. If they'd seen you and what had happened..." I shrugged.

Her voice was soft as she said, "You thought I'd be punished for destroying those books."

"Punished?" I snorted. "We both know they would have killed you for being a witch." And I wouldn't allow that to happen.

She stared at me. "You were protecting me. You didn't actually want me out of your life."

"What a stupid thing to think," I blurted, perhaps more vehemently than necessary.

She hung her head. "I might have misunderstood."

"I'd say that went beyond misunderstanding. I never saw you again." And had my heart crushed.

Dottie rolled a shoulder. "I was young and freaked-out. You yelled. I reacted."

"By leaving town that same day?"

"Did I mention I might have overreacted?"

I crossed my arms, not willing to give her a free pass. "I heard you eloped with your sister's betrothed."

She winced. "I did. Not one of my wisest decisions, but not the worst. Gerard ended up being a good husband."

"Well, good for Gerard," I said with a sneer. It burned to realize that I'd lost her over a silly misunderstanding.

"You're angry."

"You thought the worst of me." I towered over her.

She stretched up on her tiptoes, her eyes still that flashing brilliant green that haunted my memories. "Maybe if you'd not been a dick and said more than basically get out, I would have known."

"How could you not have known given I worshipped the ground you walked on?"

"You never told me," Dottie shouted back. "Never once showed me any indication."

"Like hell, I never showed you. I did everything I could." In the only way I knew how—by finding special books for her. Mustering the confidence to accept her casual invitations to dinner. Sometimes taking hours to gather the courage.

"Showing me would have been stealing a kiss, or saying, 'Dottie, I like you. Marry me.'"

"Did you know me at all?" I snapped. Seeing it from her perspective, there was shy, and then there was me. I'd been such a timid fucker back then.

"I did know you, which was why I wasn't surprised when I thought you were upset about the book and not happy to see me."

How could she not know that seeing her was always the highlight of my day? And when I lost her... I spent a long time buried in the stacks, learning to come to grips with my new demon self and my broken heart.

"Just so we're clear,"—I eyed her—"I always wanted to see you. I went to see you that same night actually, but you were already gone."

That night still haunted me. I'd found out she eloped, and I got drunk on an epic scale. But it didn't make things better. Nothing did. Which was why when I came out of my alcoholic stupor, I accepted the deal with Lucifer.

"You never came looking when I returned," was her next weak excuse.

"You returned a married woman amidst a town in the process of evacuating. I wasn't about to torture myself like that." An admission that pinched her features.

"I really did mess things up. I'm sorry."

"So am I. Because we wasted so much time. But it's never too late to start over. Or even better. Let's skip the part we've done and move right to what should have happened a long time ago. Marry me, Dottie."

Her lips parted. "No, I will not. You're insane. You're a stranger to me."

"And I don't know you at all, either. But I want to find out. Marry me."

"No."

She stalked away. I followed.

"Why not? I retired from the library the day before this cruise. There are no books now that can keep me from you." How had she ever thought my studies more important?

"It wasn't just about the books." She rounded on me. "You never even tried. Not once did you steal a kiss or say something wildly inappropriate. And now you want me to believe you have some grand love for me? Ha. I am not that gullible. This is all part of his plan."

"What are you talking about? Whose plan?"

"Lucifer's," she hissed. "You're under a spell."

"I am?" I glanced down at my body. "I don't feel as if I'm under any power."

"It must be subtle because I can't see it either. But trust me, it's there."

My lips quirked. "You think it's a spell making me say these things."

"I highly doubt you want to marry me. If you have some unrequited love fantasy, you would have looked me up ages ago. My husband has been dead a long time."

"I didn't know you were single. Once I found out you'd married, I never looked for you again." Not entirely true. I'd heard about the birth of her daughter and sent—without a return name or address —a book of children's fables. The violent, blood-thirsty kind, unlike the pale versions of modern day.

"Proving my point. You only suddenly recalled this unrequited love for me when we saw each other because it triggered a spell. You didn't happen to see Lucifer today, did you?" Dottie asked.

"Maybe. But only for a moment. He didn't cast any magic."

"As if you'd know." She snorted. "The dark lord is subtler than people give him credit for."

"I know what he's capable of." What she didn't appear to grasp was that I'd always been in love with her. I'd tried having other women in my life, none lasted long because I'd yet to meet another who could compare to Dottie. "And exactly why would Lucifer want us to be in love?"

"Who knows. Shits and giggles are enough sometimes for him. So long as you understand that what you feel isn't real."

"What if I like it and want it to be real?"

She didn't reply to that. The flare of her nostrils was the only outward sign that she actually heard me. "Tell me more about the spell on your nephew."

"I thought you couldn't break it."

"I can't, but I'm wondering if there's a way to work with it."

Despite knowing the futility, I told her everything I'd learned, mostly because I wanted to keep her around a little longer. Her prickly nature was to be expected. We'd been apart a while, and over a stupid pretext. It would take time to build a level of rapport. Or at least a few more drinks.

"The library of Atlantis might have something for you," she mused aloud. "I wonder if we could create a counter spell. Or what if the conditions are impossible to meet? Does it say what happens if the Farseer line dies out before the Kraken one?"

Because if there existed no source, then there could be no curse.

"Already suggested that to Ian. He refused to murder them. Bloody kid has a streak of good in him. It's why it's a shame he's so screwed."

"Don't give up." Dottie put her hand on mine, a subtle gesture she probably thought nothing of, yet both of our gazes were drawn to the spot where our skin touched.

I felt it. The awareness of her drew my gaze to find her staring back. "It really is nice to see you, Dottie." The dumbest, most honest thing I could say.

"I should go."

She practically ran away.

Yet I smiled. Because the lady doth protest too much.

4

DOROTHY: MARRY ME, INDEED. IT'S TOO LATE FOR US.

THERE MUST BE a way for me to not feel so out of control around Shax. At my age, I should have a better grip. Yet I felt intimidated around him, and not because he dominated me in a patriarchal fashion. It was more I felt...disadvantaged. There he was, young and virile, tempting me into sin. Acting as if my old flesh were some desirable thing.

Not fair. Shax should suffer as much as I. I glanced down at my body. It had served me well, but the joints grew tired, the naps longer, a result of staying in character.

It was time to shed the disguise.

On my way back to my room, I ran into a shifter in the hall by my door. All that sniffing around made it obvious that he was looking for Jane. I sent him packing. If he was still that interested, then let him find my granddaughter in the morning.

The same went for Shax. What would he do when he saw me? Because I had no doubt that he'd hunt me down.

He'd have a surprise when he did. I turned back the clock on my appearance, shedding more than twenty years to make myself just a touch younger maybe than Shax chose to appear. It certainly took my granddaughter by surprise. But Shax didn't bat an eye when he saw me.

Didn't remark once on the change. The demi-demon did, however, remain glued to me, sitting beside me at breakfast, distracting me from spying on Jane and that shifter who had indeed tracked her down.

The damned demi-demon followed me after the morning meal as I kept an eye on my granddaughter, who'd chosen to go for a swim. Probably heard me haranguing Jane, on purpose, mostly to make sure the lion shifter's family didn't cause trouble. They hadn't been impressed to find my Jane kissing their king.

The entire morning, Shax had stayed in the background, not talking to me, not interfering. Just there constantly, despite how I tried to lose him.

And why was I trying to lose him and in turn

shirking my duty to Lucifer? The dark lord had asked me to spy on Shax. I should thank the fact that the demi-demon actually aided me with his stalking.

By the noon hour, I instead snapped, "Are you done following me already?" Why did Shax have to be so aggressively masculine? What'd happened to the shy boy I used to boss around?

"Who says I'm following you? Maybe you're the one following me," he said as he came to a stop by my stool at the bar. He looked handsome in his casual suit, the tan slacks matching the jacket, his mauve shirt buttoned but open at the neck. The hat proved to be an elegant touch.

"I was here first." Just like I'd been first to yoga class where he lounged, watching from behind his glasses. I swung around on the stool, the height enough to bring me eye-level with his chin.

"Physically, perhaps, but I thought about coming here before you did," he countered. "Really, Dottie. Reading my mind to find out my plan. I didn't know you'd gotten so strong."

I gritted my teeth. "You are impossible."

"In what sense? Because I obviously exist. If you meant that I can't be pleased, then I can assure you, it won't take much. I'm a simple man with simple pleasures." His gaze dropped to my mouth.

I moistened my lips with the tip of my tongue. "I don't remember you being a stalker."

"You want me to leave?"

"Yes."

"Then I'll go." He rose.

I said one word. "Don't."

He sat back down. The bartender slid a drink in front of him. For a moment, we said nothing, then we both spoke at once.

"Your granddaughter—"

"Your nephew—"

We both stopped.

He smiled. "You first."

"I saw your nephew in the water."

"The curse is forcing him into it every few hours." His lips turned down. "It won't be long now. At least your granddaughter appears to be doing well."

I frowned. "Don't be so sure. She's a stubborn one. It took a lot of my power to imbue that locket with enough magic to make it work." It left me depleted, another reason I'd needed an ocean trip. Some people recharged their magical batteries by resting. For me, being on the ocean revived me the quickest.

"What will you do once she doesn't need you?"

I snorted. "Anything I want."

"Alone?"

I eyed him. "I've been alone for a while."

"I've been alone forever," he admitted.

"That's not a reason for people to be together."

"You know it's not the only one." Shax reached for my hand, and I let him hold it.

The tingles were something I'd not felt in a long, long time. "This isn't real." I don't know if I said it for myself or him.

"You keep saying that. Why?" Shax asked.

"I told you, the devil cast a spell."

A crowd of people entered the bar suddenly, and the noise level jumped.

Shax leaned close and whispered against my ear, "What I feel isn't a spell. Get used to it."

Then he left.

Didn't steal a kiss. Or cop a feel. Just made a promise. It affected me more than any touch.

Only once Shax disappeared from the room did I dare hiss, "Lucifer. If you're listening, we need to talk."

Despite the raucous noise, the dark lord replied as if he stood right beside me. "What do you want to talk about? Is it about your unrequited lust for me? Because I'm afraid I'll have to disappoint. I'm a one-wench demon at the moment."

I whirled. "For the millionth time, I don't want to sleep with you."

"You keep telling yourself that." The devil winked. I took a moment to ingest his unique style.

He'd changed since our last visit and now sported board shorts patterned with a rather dirty-looking octopus, each appendage in the shape of a male endowment. His white shirt held hundreds of sloppy-looking white spots. The implication proved a bit...in your face.

I glanced at my drink and the condensation on the side of the glass rather than the eyesore. "The love spell you put on Shax is too strong. Take it off. Tone it down. Do something. Because he is driving me nuts." I stopped short of saying that it made me feel things. Stuff I'd thought myself long past.

"How utterly romantic," Lucifer crooned. "The way you're fighting your affection for him. Making this situation unnecessarily angsty."

"There is no *situation*," I growled.

He clapped his hands. "Not yet. But I can see one coming." He sang the words, and I heard the threat.

I glared at him. "Take the spell off."

"Can't."

"You will!" I shouted, losing control of myself for a moment.

"I can't remove it because there is no spell."

Lucifer smirked and tucked his hands behind his back.

"You're lying."

"For once, I am telling the ugly truth. No spell. My head librarian likes you. Which I think makes him certifiable, but that's his nightmare, not mine. Deal with it."

"I thought Shax retired."

"He doesn't know it yet, but I refused his resignation. None of those peons under him are ready for that exalted position."

My lips pursed. "It's for a keeper of books."

"Which only shows how little you know," Lucifer muttered with disdain.

"What's that supposed to mean?"

"Just that you're not as smart as you think."

"And neither are you, oh paranoid one. Shax isn't plotting against you." The man might be many things, but a traitor wasn't one of them.

"Shows how little you know, because even now, he's secretly meeting with my wife." Lucifer leaned close and growled, a thin tendril of smoke rising from a nostril. "And you're here moping about your task because he still makes your panties wet. Do your job, witch. Find out what he's up to with my wench."

When the devil spoke quietly, you moved.

But what to do when I found myself outside Shax's door? Should I knock? Barge in? What would I say? What excuse could I use?

I wasted time staring at the door. I'd figure something out. I knocked, and it took only a moment before he answered. I shoved past him, drawn by the lingering aroma of fresh flowers on a spring breeze.

I scanned the empty room and noted the perfectly made bed before my gaze turned to Shax and registered the fact that he only wore a towel. And he looked... Wow.

5

SHAX: THAT BOOK ON WITCHES REALLY NEEDS A BIGGER WARNING ABOUT PISSING THEM OFF.

"LOOKING FOR SOMETHING?" I asked as Dottie stared at me. Kind of gratifying, actually.

Her gaze snapped away from me, and her brow wrinkled. She sniffed. "Am I interrupting?" she asked all too sweetly. "I didn't realize you had company."

"Just me."

"I thought I heard voices."

A lie because Mother Nature would have secured the room against eavesdropping. "Can't a man have a conversation with himself?" I closed the door to the hall.

"What are you doing?"

"I didn't realize we wanted to have our conversation with everyone on the ship." I took a step away from the door, and she held her ground in the middle of the room. She also studiously ignored my chest. A little too intently compared to the staring of before.

"What are you doing, Shax?" she asked.

"I was about to take a shower."

"Before that. I can smell perfume."

Young me would have gaped stupidly at her and stuttered that, of course, I wasn't doing anything. However, Mother Nature had just left. The scent of her probably lingered, and Dottie sure didn't seem happy about it.

"You want us to be exclusive, you just say the word."

"Don't play games with me." Dottie's hair danced on a magical wind, lifting and twisting, while her eyes stormed with dark, cresting waves. Freaky and hot all at once.

I stepped farther away from the door. Not to get clothes, though. I entered the bathroom and turned on the shower, wondering at the timing of Dottie's arrival.

We'd parted not long ago—on her terms I might add—yet here she was at my door, looking like a cat dunked in cold water, all hissing and spitting-mad. A little earlier, and she might have caught me with Gaia.

Mother Nature had returned to rant about how Lucifer appeared suspicious. Sprinkled admonishments that I needed to be careful. She also made me promise not to tell Lucifer a thing. A vow that would never count since Lucifer already suspected that she was playing around.

"This has nothing to do with us but the woman you had here." To my surprise, Dottie followed me to the bathroom door. She leaned against the frame and crossed her arms.

"You keep saying it has nothing to do with us, yet every word out of your mouth sounds jealous. How long you going to keep pretending you don't care?" I turned to the shower.

"I don't," she grumbled. "As an old friend, I'm concerned about your choice."

"And just who do you think I'm seeing romantically?" I reached in and felt the water. Hot.

"Was it Gaia, you dumb idiot?"

"Dumb?" I questioned her choice of words even as she had a point. Gaia acted indiscreetly, and Dottie had the astuteness to notice. I trod very carefully. "That would be insane. No one would dare mess with the dark lord's wife."

"One would hope not, given that anyone who did would probably die."

"It touches me to know you are worried about my health." My hand went to the waistband of the towel.

"I don't care," she growled, looking adorable. And much younger.

I had to wonder at the change in her appearance since last night. She'd shown up this morning smooth-skinned with her hair that stunning jet color I remembered and curly beyond belief. So utterly beautiful, smart, and confident. She also seemed rather convinced that I was under a charm of some kind. As if a love spell could be to blame for how I felt.

Adorable how she refused to accept the truth. I'd loved her for a long time.

"I was just about to shower. Care to join?" I tugged the cloth free. The modest boy of long ago with his pasty skin and no abs hadn't existed in a while. Keeping the library safe had turned out to be more my style than constantly having my nose buried in books. I kept in shape now. Traveled throughout Hell and to other planes, looking for rare knowledge to bring back to the library. Some-times, that information came with legs, too many eyes, and required a cell with a keeper. The library didn't discriminate on the forms that knowledge could take.

The towel hit the floor. I caught her gaze and held it as I stepped into the steaming-hot water. "Shower is big enough for two."

To my surprise, she stalked towards me, then stopped with a smirk. Her fingers waggled, and the water turned ice-cold.

I lost male status in that frigid moment. An indignant bellow emerged as I jumped out. I glared as I grabbed my towel and scrubbed at my skin.

"That was mean."

Her eyes sparkled. "For you. But fun for me."

"Good to know." My own magic flicked, and the shower sprayed her.

She opened her mouth and screeched, "You jerk!"

I let the water return to the shower and smiled at her soggy self. "You're right. That was fun."

A hand skimmed down her body and sluiced the water to the floor. She glared at me, then broke into a chuckle. In moments, she was laughing hard. "You are not that shy librarian anymore, are you?"

"Nope. Just like you're not a junior witch. Rumor has it you're pretty badass."

She rolled a shoulder and offered a preening smile. "I do all right."

I wound the towel around my waist before approaching her. "I wasn't kidding before. I'd like to get to know the new you."

"You might not like her," she said softly, staring at me.

"Actually, I am thinking that I might like her quite a bit."

Dottie stood framed in the doorway, so I bracketed the opening with a hand on each side. I leaned into her, bending down to bring our faces close.

"You are much too cocky for my liking."

"I would have said just cocky enough." I leaned in and kissed her.

We both had our eyes open, Dottie's wide. I tasted her immediate surprise as she drew in a sharp breath.

I winked. And whispered, "Kiss me back."

"No."

"Weren't you the one saying I never took the initiative?"

"It's too late now."

"Are you sure?" I said, pulling back a bit so only my breath fluttered over her lips.

"I don't even know if I like you," she grumbled, yanking me back and pressing her mouth to mine. She kissed me, and not just a quick peck.

Her lips were soft and plush as they explored mine. Teasing me, tasting me, her hands roaming my body, skimming over my skin. Grabbing my ass through the towel.

She reminded me what if felt like to be a young

man enraptured by a woman to the point where the barest touch enflamed.

When Dottie pulled away, she left me panting. My body was flushed with arousal, and the towel fell, pulled free by my erection.

She appeared only a little disheveled as she eyed me. "Do you always look like that after a kiss?"

As if my world exploded? "What do you think?" I growled. Did she yet understand just how much she affected me?

Apparently not, because she said, "If this is your standard kissing face, then at least you are not fooling around with Lucifer's wife."

The very idea had me losing my happy vibe and saying, "Excuse me?"

"I had to know for sure. And it seems you were telling the truth because your kissing face is nothing like your oh-shit-I-almost-got-caught face."

I gaped at her. "You kissed me as a test?"

"Just making sure you weren't being dumb."

"Where would you even get the idea that I was sleeping with Gaia?"

"People talk."

"No one is talking, because no one but you knows she was here. And how did you even...?" I groaned. "Lucifer. Don't tell me he's harassing you, too."

"When isn't he being a demanding devil?"

"What does he want from you?"

"I told you, he's matchmaking again." She snorted. "Me and you. As if that would work."

"Don't be so sure that's what he wants. When your precious lord visited me, he didn't say anything to me about you. He just told me to keep an eye out for hinky shit."

"Hinkier than your nephew turning monster of the deep?" Dottie queried, the note of it high-pitched. "The boy almost drowned my Jane this morning."

I winced. "Ian's having a tough time. Turns out he married a woman last night. A Farseer, as a matter of fact."

Dottie stared a moment before exclaiming, "He broke the curse!"

"Not quite. Marriage is only part of it. She needs to love him, too."

"I have a spell that can help with that," she mused aloud.

I shook my head. "Can't be magic. It has to be real."

"I know," she muttered. "Curses are a delicate thing to play with. Could do more harm than good. But there must be a loophole. Maybe I could peek at him again."

"I'll see if I can arrange it. Ian's been hard to track down of late. When he's not off being a kraken, I think the plan is to woo his wife." I kept hoping it would be enough, but he was running out of time, and the curse had yet to show signs of faltering.

"What were Lucifer's exact orders to you?" Dottie asked, choosing to sit in a chair, putting herself out of reach.

Since my nudity wasn't sending her into flaming puddles of desire, I went for clothes.

"I told you, I am supposed to watch for weird shit. He thinks there's something bad coming to get him."

"There's always something bad coming to get him. If he's tired of it, he should learn to delegate more," Dottie remarked.

"His daughter handled a few catastrophes threatening the nine circles recently."

"She's been acting as his general on the battlefield. Not the same as running the Pit."

"She did step in once."

"Only because Lucifer went cuckoo for a bit." Dottie swirled a finger. "Way I hear it, his daughter vowed...never again."

"She's not the only one who's tried. He did abdicate his throne for a while there when his fake son took over as King of Hell." I pulled on some swim shorts.

"Didn't last, though, did it? The devil enjoys his work."

"Don't let him hear you say that." Lucifer was likely to have Dottie silenced before someone overheard.

The witch smirked. "Don't you worry about me. The Lord of Hell and I have an understanding. Which is why I agreed to keep an eye on you."

I paused before grabbing a shirt. "Keep an eye on me? Those are your orders?"

"The devil thinks you're plotting against him and told me to stick close."

"That explains why you came running to my room. And here I thought it was because you wanted to say yes to my proposal."

"I am not marrying you. I am here because Lucifer knows you're meeting with his wife."

"I had a feeling he did. What did he say? Did it end with 'off with Shax's head?'"

"You're not going to deny it?" Dottie eyed me, looking rather cross.

"Nope." I buttoned the shirt, only three of the fasteners, just enough to keep it from fluttering.

"Why are you meeting Gaia in your room?" Dottie snapped. She cleared her throat. "I mean,

Lucifer wants to know what reason you could possibly have for meeting his wife in secret."

"Not doing what your jealous eyes are accusing me of, that's for sure," I retorted.

She tilted her chin. "This isn't jealousy."

"So you wouldn't lose your shit if you found out I was giving her a hand? Doing my best to please a goddess?"

The color in Dottie's cheeks amused, but before she could explode and sink the ship, I chuckled. "Relax. I'm helping her with a bit of research."

"Don't you need a library for that?"

"I do. But not the one in Hell. The tidbit I'm looking for is in Atlantis."

"If she's only doing research, then why is she sneaking around?"

"Because."

Dorothy's gaze narrowed. "What exactly is she searching for?"

"I am not at liberty to say."

"Must be bad if she won't tell Lucifer."

"She's worried he'll overreact."

Dottie sighed. "Oh, crap on a stick. She's doing something to protect him, which means when he finds out, he'll be split between being pissed that she's babying him, and maudlin because she loves him so much."

"Bingo." I nodded. "She's trying to prevent another of his mood swings." The devil had been going through quite a few since he hit a certain epic milestone birthday.

"And she thought sneaking around with another male would be better than telling him the truth?" Dottie snorted. "Lucifer is a powder keg set to go off. So, do yourself a favor and tell me what's going on. What does she want you to find?"

"I can't tell you because you'll just run back to Lucifer."

"I will not," she huffed. She lied.

I shook my head. "You are his minion. Tonight is the solstice, and I already know you'll be dancing naked for him." I'd learned about witches over the centuries. Curious about the one I'd lost.

"I'm a witch. It's expected of me."

"It's old-fashioned."

"Maybe I like being old-fashioned." She tossed her head.

"If you were old-fashioned, you'd be married and wearing a skirt." I paused. "To your ankles."

Her lips rounded. "That is sexist."

"And you are modern. As am I. I would prefer to know you're dancing naked around a fire because you want to."

"That's just it, though. I do like it. The freedom in

having the air kiss my skin. The heat of the flames licking it. The decadence of it and embracing life. It's fun. You should try it."

"Are you asking me to come dance naked by the light of the moon with you?" I arched a brow. "I accept."

She squeaked. "I was only saying that in jest."

"I am quite serious."

"You'll be the only man. The warlocks think they're above that kind of thing. It's why witches can be stronger. The dark lord blesses us for the gift."

"Are you trying to uninvite me? Because that's rude, which I guess is being done on purpose to please your lord, so I can choose to ignore your uninvite and just crash your naked bonfire party. Should I bring anything? Drinks? A joint?"

"You aren't acting at all as expected." Her lips turned down.

"And that's frustrating you."

"Yes!" She made a sound of annoyance, almost a growl. She popped out of the chair and approached me, jabbing at my chest. "You are not the Shax I knew."

"I'm version five point six, Dottie." I'd had to reinvent myself a few times before finding the me that fit best.

"You're impossible."

"I think the correct term is unique."

She stood poised in front of me, close enough that I could grab her for a kiss. Near enough for a slap if she didn't like it. Instead, I waited.

What would she do?

"I need to go get ready for the fire tonight."

"How long does it take to strip?" I asked.

"Well, considering I like to ensure all the hair on my body is gone..." She looked down at herself. At the vee of her legs.

I might have stopped breathing.

While I remained frozen, she left.

But I knew where she'd be later—and utterly bare. I just didn't expect to be delayed on the way there.

My other nephew, Adexios, captain of the *Sushi Lover*, renowned for his mishaps at sea, came looking for me after dinner. "Uncle Shax, I need a hand with something."

"Did Ian wreck a piece of the ship?" While Killian used to have great control of his kraken, as the permanent change neared, the beast got stronger.

"No, he's fine. We did have a little incident with a passenger this morning during the swim, but she's not pressing charges."

It reminded me of what Dottie had said earlier.

"What happened? Who did Ian almost drown? Please don't tell me it was his wife."

My nephew had pulled a squid out of his ass and managed to marry a Farseer, one of the few who could break his curse. Now if only they would fall in love for real in the next twenty-four hours, he'd be free.

"Everyone is fine. We have a love-spelled locket on the loose, causing a bit of craziness. But Dorothy swears it won't cause any permanent harm."

Wait, Dottie had cast a love spell? For whom? "I can help you find it."

"Maybe later. The problem I have is… Better I just show you. Come with me."

Curious, I followed my nephew even as the moon rose. By the baying howls and the smell of smoke, the solstice and full moon festivities had begun —without me.

Surely, I could wrap up Adexios's problem and still make it to the naked bonfire dancing part of the evening.

We descended the many levels of the ship, using a utility elevator not available to guests. It went down, down, and then down some more. We stopped a level before the water zone for the passengers who needed more than a tub of H2O for their needs.

The tops of numerous pools shimmered, the

waters cloudy with a film to provide privacy to those inside. From a far pool, a selkie heaved himself to the perforated deck, dripping water and swapping his seal skin for human. He rose and snared a robe from a hook, compliments of the ship.

"When are you going to start explaining?"

"Soon. I don't want the others"—Adexios eyed the selkie and smiled as he walked past—"to know."

"Sounds ominous."

"I wouldn't have bugged you otherwise."

Adexios waited until we passed the guest quarters and moved through a locked door to another section. The pools in this area were mostly covered in grates. Prisoners or catch of the day?

"He was discovered by the chefs when they came to pick out some fish for dinner. We moved him to an empty vat." Adexios pointed to the far end.

"Who was discovered?"

"Some kind of fish man. He won't say who he is or where he comes from. Sweets has been trying to get him to talk, but she's not had any luck."

"Sweets is here?" I brightened at the news. The sea monster had taken Adexios as a pet. Kind of a first. Given Ian's impending dilemma, I'd brought him around for a visit, introduced them. Maybe having a friend when he turned all sea monster and had to live in the Styx would help.

An eyeball on a purple stalk rose from the only open pool and blinked at me.

"Hello, gorgeous. How has my favorite girl been?" I drawled.

The eye craned for me, and I gave her soft lid and lashes a rub. "When are you going to ditch my nephew and come live in my pond?" I asked. "I just bought a bubble jet for it."

The rapid blinks purred the lashes over my skin.

"Stop trying to steal my sea monster," Adexios grumbled. "She's mine." A reminder that had Sweets bolting for Adexios and wrapping him in a hug. The man still had the ability to blush. "Love you too, Sweets. Now, business time. Show Shax our prisoner."

The eyestalk whipped over to the tank beside hers. I joined it and peeked down into the water. It didn't have the oily sheen for privacy blocking my view, only a grate secured with a thick padlock. I saw a man sitting at the bottom of the vat. A fish man, his body hairless, a fin mohawking the top of his head, more fins around his arms and the backs of his legs.

"You said you found him in a tank with other fish. Could he have gotten there by accident with a catch?"

Adexios shook his head. "Each one was specifically handpicked to ensure only quality seafood for the length of the trip."

"So, he snuck in after." I knelt down and observed the prisoner's lack of clothing. The legs weren't fused together, and yet I could tell he kept his genitals tucked away. "Male, but not a merman. Not a pure one, at any rate." Could be a hybrid. They had a tendency to favor one parent over the other, but later generations tended to have more mixed characteristics.

"I figured that due to the lack of a tail. But given his appearance, I'm going to make a guess and say he's from Atlantis," Adexios stated.

I nodded. "Seems most likely. They're the only ones on record who have this kind of blending of aquatic and human traits." The tattoo on the fish man's chest also gave it away. An inverted trident pattern.

"Why would an Atlantean hide with our catch?"

"Spying, obviously. The question is what, or who, is he spying on? Is he just watching the cruise, trying to ensure that no one tries anything when we dock on his island? Is he looking for information on a particular guest? Or is he part of an effort to sabotage?"

"Why would anyone sabotage? Have they not heard of me? It's bound to happen before the cruise is over." Adexios knew his limitations. His father Charon might be the greatest boatman known in all the planes, but alas, his son didn't inherit that gene. Still, my nephew kept trying.

"I hear they won't let you near the controls for the ship."

Adexios nodded. "They figure if I'm captain in name only, we might not run aground or get pulverized by a storm."

"You do realize you have witches, demons, a kraken, and a shit ton of other magical folk aboard, right?"

"If only they were enough to stop what will surely happen," Adexios said with a mournful shake of his head.

"Don't be such a pessimist. It doesn't always end in a ship sinking."

"Do we need to list the ways it can go wrong?" Adexios exclaimed, flinging his hands above his head. "Or have you forgotten our family vacation?" He turned his gaze on me. "Remember the swan ride at the amusement park?"

I did. The chain had suddenly gotten caught, and everyone got dumped into what had turned out to be a baby-alligator-infested pond.

"You still whining about that? Those little teeth were no worse than a nipple clamp." Valaska laughed as she joined us, the sound boisterous just like the rest of her. Think tall, wide, and blond with some Viking blood, and you'd have Adexios's wife. The complete opposite of him, and yet theirs was a love match. She was also the *Sushi Lover*'s head of security.

Her and Adexios's match had resulted in children. A pair of tiny robed beings who currently stood wraithlike by Valaska's side. Cory and Kelly. My great-nephews or nieces. It was never actually specified.

I held open my arms. "Come say hi to your uncle." I no longer feared little people since raising Ian.

When I rose, I had a child perched on each hip, their weight pleasing, their fingers clutching the treats they knew I kept in my pockets. A man should always have something sweet within reach. A trick all librarians learned early on.

The cowls of their robes hid their faces, but not their new size. "You've grown."

"We are getting strong on the blood of our enemies," Cory stated.

"You sound like your mother."

"They both like to bash things," Valaska confided.

"And what do you prefer, Kelly?" I asked.

"Books."

"A child of knowledge." My heart swelled with joy.

Then popped.

"I don't read them. I eat them. With peanut butter and jelly. Mom says its 'cause I've got special dietary needs."

"That's weird," whispered Cory. "Everyone knows you have PB and J on steak."

They were both delightfully strange. A perfect fit to the family.

Valaska leaned over the tank. "When are you gonna let me question him?"

That led to a big sigh from Adexios. "We discussed this. You don't understand fish men."

"Leave me Sweets to translate. I'll get him to talk." Adexios's blood-thirsty wife belonged to the Amazonians, a rough bunch of women who'd carved out a spot of their own in Hell that even Lucifer didn't step foot in.

"How about you all leave, and I have a chat with the fellow?" I said pleasantly. I handed the children off to Adexios. The tiny people in the robes grumbled before snuggling their dad.

"I can stay and help," Valaska offered.

"Afraid I'm going to have to call special privilege on this one," I said with a shake of my head.

"You think this fellow might have information that affects Hell?" Adexios didn't hide his skepticism.

"Yes."

"I thought Lucifer wasn't allowed to screw around on Earth because of the treaty with his brother." Adexios rolled a child to his back to hang on monkey-style, while the other remained curled in his arm. He always kept one hand free these days. He'd finally learned that danger could lurk anywhere.

"The situation appears to not be of his making. He's just keeping an eye out as it might affect Hell."

"Whatever it is, don't sink the ship. I'll never hear the end of it," Adexios grumbled as he stalked off.

Valaska paused. "Are you sure?"

"I've got Sweets if I run into trouble."

The sea monster wagged its bobble eye. I kept a benign smile on my face as I watched my nephew and his family leave. Only once the door shut did the expression drop as I turned to the tank.

Atlantis had sent a spy. Not good. They'd been sunk for misbehaving centuries ago. I would have thought they'd learned their lesson.

I looked at Sweets. "I'm guessing you told Adexios to fetch me."

The eye bobbled.

"Good thinking. That tattoo on his chest? Means

he's part of King Rex's elite guard." King Rex being the current warlord in charge of Atlantis. Which meant the spy probably didn't have a tongue, so he couldn't talk. Audibly, at any rate.

The king could speak mind-to-mind with his loyal subjects. His guards being the most steadfast. Having their tongues removed was part of that honor. If they got caught, they couldn't reveal a thing.

As we'd already conjectured, there could be many reasons King Rex had sent a spy. Keeping an eye on the maiden voyage to his shores. Perhaps we provided an easy passage back for a soldier returning from his mission. Or did this spy have an interest in someone on board?

Atlantis had been known to steal people before in the interest of keeping their bloodlines from stagnating. But I didn't burden Adexios with that knowledge. He had enough to handle already.

The eyestalk skimmed the water and agitated the fish man. The prisoner took a few swipes that Sweets dodged. She returned to blink wetly at me.

"No weapons on him?" Interesting. "Could they be hidden somewhere that he could access if he got out of the tank?"

Sweets bobbed around, looking.

I chuckled. "Don't worry, sweetheart. He won't

be getting out of this tank to use them. We are going to need some help cracking open his head to read his thoughts, though." I could probably find a psychic or two on board. Heck, Ian was now married to a seer. Maybe Sasha could read minds too. Problem being I couldn't have just anyone privy to the secrets we might reveal. I needed someone I could trust.

"You watch over him while I fetch someone who can help us."

The stalk plumped with pride and glared at the cell's water surface.

I used the utility elevator to get to the roof in time to still catch some of the fire dancing. Naked bodies moved to music only they could hear. Young and old, all shapes and sizes, but I only had eyes for one. Her body was rounded in a Venus shape, full-hipped and breasted, her expression alight with joy.

Something I used to see when she came to visit me at the library. Happiness she'd exhibited the last time I saw her when she kissed me before everything went to shit. How could I have been so blind? So shy. So stupid. She could have been mine for the taking.

Odd how I'd been in love with Dorothy for so long and yet had never seen her naked. And now, my first time, she writhed for the devil.

It didn't seem right to stare, and so I put my back to the dancing, resisting the temptation. I remained with my back to them even after I knew they were done. I waited for Dottie to join me by the rail. Her face shone with perspiration, her robe loosely belted.

"What happened to dancing naked by the moon?" she teased.

"Was afraid someone would laugh at my dangly bits bouncing, and they'd shrivel so far I'd never see them again."

The ribald jest took her by surprise. I could see it, but then laughter shook her, a rich and throaty sound.

"I can't believe you just joked about turtling."

"I can't believe you laughed instead of slapping me."

Her lips curved. "Did you know my granddaughter thinks me a bit of a prude?"

"You?" I shook my head. "I heard a rumor you were the one who began the whole naked coven dancing thing back in the day."

"It got the dark lord's attention much better than the chicken sacrifices." Her white teeth gleamed.

"Speaking of the dark lord, I need your help with something."

"If you say your zipper, I will toss you off the ship."

"I shouldn't have to ask. If you want it, you know how to get at it."

"Sexy. It's a wonder I can keep my clothes on," was her dry reply.

"When I am seducing you, you'll know it." I winked. "But that's not why I'm here. Can I borrow you for something?"

"What for?"

"I can't say. Too many eyes and ears. I can only show you."

Her eyebrow arched. "You're not helping here."

"I promise it's not sexual. But it is wet." I couldn't help that last bit.

Once more, I got a deep laugh. "I'm curious, old man. Lead the way."

"Old?" I arched a brow. "Anytime you want to test my stamina…"

"It's not about stamina but skill," she purred.

The challenge was almost too much to bear. I might have done something about it then and there, except I had another priority. Did the presence of a spy mean danger to the ship?

I couldn't relax and seduce her until I knew for sure. I guided Dottie down to the fish man's cell. However, I didn't think to warn her about Sweets.

The eyestalk bobbed in front of Dorothy. It glared.

"Don't move," I advised in a low tone, noticing Sweets' jealousy.

"This is your big problem?" Dottie asked. "A machete should take care of it."

Sweets blinked rapidly.

"She doesn't mean it, sweetheart." I soothed the monster. "No one is cutting off your beautiful stalk."

"Are you baby-talking the eyeball?" muttered Dottie.

"You might want to be nice around Sweets," I suggested in an almost whisper. Then to the sea monster, I said, "This is Dottie, an old friend. Who was just joking and promises to be nice."

The stalk wound around me to glare.

"You don't have to like her," I said, "but she can help us crack into our prisoner's head and see what goodies he's hiding inside."

The tentacle wavered and fluttered its lashes some more.

I shook my head. "No, you may not crack his head to see what's inside. Your methods will kill him."

The stalk drooped.

"Be a good girl, and you can have him when we're done." The eyeball straightened. "Will you bring him to the bars so Dottie can touch him?"

"Don't know what you expect me to do. I might

have magic, but I can't read minds," Dorothy stated.

"I know you can't, which is why I want you to scry instead."

"That requires a focus object. Is he wearing something I can use?"

"Nope. All we have is the fish man himself."

Dottie pursed her lips. "I admit, I've never tried it with a living thing before. I don't know what effect it will have on him."

"Meaning?"

"Loss of mental cognition. Possible bodily combustion. The creation of a temporal rip that allows an alien entity to possess it and infiltrate our world."

"Yadda. Yadda. The bottom line is you can use him to scry."

"More than likely."

"Will you do it?" I took the time to ask.

"What happens if I say no?"

I rolled my shoulders. "Then I'll see if I can find someone else on board who can help me. Hopefully, they don't hear anything untoward that forces me to kill them."

"Still protecting that secret."

"Protecting the dark lord from things he doesn't want to hear protects us all."

A sigh escaped Dottie. "True."

"Will you do it?"

"Of course, I will. Just give me a second to gather some supplies."

It took more than a few seconds to find everything we needed. More like a few hours. Huge bag of salt. Black candles, which proved hard to locate since the witches aboard were hoarding them for sex magic rituals.

I could only stand by and watch as Dottie created a large circle on the catwalk around the vat, dribbling salt in an oval rather than a circular shape. She used more salt to create a pentagram with candles at each point. Once done, she sat crossed-legged in it, bowed her head, and said, "Okay, I'm ready. Bring him to the surface so I can touch him with the spell."

Sweets darted into the water, but only when she went to wind herself around the Atlantean did he react. His webbed fingers slashed—extending previously hidden claws—and a ribbon of blood stained the water as he scored the sea monster's flesh.

"Sweets!" I made to go to her aid.

Dorothy hissed, "Don't you dare break my circle."

I could only watch as the tentacle curved into the cell, agitated. Sweets didn't make a sound, but her pool of water trembled, and the water in the fish man's cell got rough, too rough to see.

When it cleared, Sweets had the Atlantean

wrapped in a noose and yanked so his face pressed into the grate.

"Aren't you just a lovely and tough gal," Dorothy crooned. "I can see why Shax is fond of you."

The water in Sweets' vat shivered.

"Don't steal my sea monster."

"Afraid she'll like me more?" Dottie winked. "Sea witches have an affinity with the ocean's creatures."

Librarians, too.

Dorothy turned serious and reached out for the fish man. She placed her hand on his cheek and hissed some words.

I sensed more than saw the summoning of magic. Scrying, contrary to what some might believe, was a difficult thing to cast. Throwing air as a weapon or shaping water as a tool, those had form and required just the will to make them happen. Scrying meant capturing the resonance of something, going in blind to pull on the miasma that surrounded things both alive and not. Digging into the unknown, uncovering memories. An inert object was difficult. Retrieving from a mind that was not receptive to intrusion…that took some mad skill.

A cold wind blew through the room, rippling the hair, swirling into a mist over the body. It hung there. Waiting.

"Ask," Dottie murmured. "Ask a question, and it

will answer."

"Why are you here?"

The reaction proved instantaneous. The fog spread out, a huge moving swatch in the air. It took on shadows, then ripples that became dimensional and colored.

An image appeared.

I saw the fish man holding a spear and kneeling in front of a throne. A flicker, then that same fellow was stealing aboard the *Sushi Lover*. Another flicker. Escaping the pens and stalking the ship.

Looking for something.

Looking for someone.

There was a disturbance in the vision, feedback that caused it to ripple and waver. The body in the water thrashed, trying to break free. When the images returned, and I looked again, we'd obviously missed a section because we saw our captive firing a corked bottle into the ocean. Sending a message about what to whom?

"What does that message say?"

The vision began to swirl—

Ploof!

The fish man's body exploded and splattered us with guts. No more questions.

I eyed Dottie through a hanging hunk of green slime. "That offer to share a shower is still open."

6

DOROTHY: IT DOESN'T MATTER HOW OLD THEY ARE, MEN ARE PERVERTS.

I SHOULD HAVE SAID yes just to see if Shax meant it. However, covered in a fish man's guts, and not feeling romantic, I shook my head.

"I'm afraid I need to be somewhere else shortly."

"What do you think we saw?" he asked.

My shoulders rolled. "Obviously, a spy for the king. Not sure what he was looking for. He had some kind of shield over that part of his memories."

"Meaning we still have no answer. I'll have to advise Adexios to be cautious."

"And while you're doing that, I'm going to check on my granddaughter."

I left Shax, knowing I'd have to hurry. I could feel the clock ticking. The cruise ship had entered DJ's Locker, the home of my daughter and son-in-law.

My dear daughter wouldn't react well to finding

her mother cheating on the memory of her father. May his soul rot in Heaven. How the man managed to remain so disgustingly good being married to me was a mystery. The only untoward thing he ever did was marry me. And there were times I wished I'd never eloped.

But then, Shax might not have grown into such a delicious example of a man.

Delicious? The very idea had me gnashing my teeth. Had I entered my horny hundreds again?

Good thing Gerard, a mortal man, had already died by then. The man had proven boring and predictable in the sack. Given Shax's intriguing new confidence, I didn't think he would leave me yawning. Just one kiss and I'd almost creamed myself. Obviously, a sign I needed to get out more often.

Quickly making it to my room, I hopped into the cramped shower. There was barely room to move around. Good thing I didn't have to shave my legs.

The lack of space didn't stop the devil from appearing, looming on the other side of the tiny frosted door.

"How come no one told me there would be Undine sushi?" he exclaimed.

"Is that what that thing was called? An Undine?"

"Judging by the smell of its guts in your hair, a variation of."

"Whatever its name, it was on board the ship, spying."

"Not very well, obviously, or he wouldn't have been caught." The devil snorted.

"It died before we could find out much. I don't suppose his soul came to you in Hell?"

Lucifer shook his head. "The Undines are interesting creatures. Possessed of some intellect, and more closely resembling the humans on the Earthen plane than any other animal. Except for one thing. Their souls don't come to me."

"They go to Heaven?" Because that was the only other place that came quickly to mind.

"Nope. They go somewhere else."

"Cool." And not entirely surprising. There were many planes out there. And different timelines. Reality could change with the killing of just one person. Not a butterfly as the mundanes liked to quote. Only grave and pivotal deaths could affect huge shifts big enough to spawn a new timeline.

In another world, I might have married Shax. Being married, would he still have chosen to become a demi-demon to save his precious library? Or would he have lived a mundane life and died an old man?

"More than likely, the Undine you killed worked for Atlantis," Lucifer announced.

"Shax already figured that out."

The devil eyed me with sudden raptor-like interest. "Of course, he did. Tell me, do you know what that old demon is up to? You haven't reported anything to me yet."

"Because there's not much to say."

"I beg to differ, seeing how often my wife,"—spoken on a growl of puffed smoke—"has popped onto this ship. To see *him*. Not me. She gets a few minutes off, and is she looking me up to show me her female parts? No. She's plotting against me."

I debated letting Lucifer froth himself into a righteous rage, but he might accidentally take it out on Shax. I'd feel bad if that happened.

"She's not cheating on you." I rinsed off the last of the soap and debated whether to keep the water on or not. I wasn't about to step out without a robe or a towel, which might sound odd. After all, I'd danced around countless bonfires in the buff while the devil watched. But that was during rituals with the coven. Alone with Lucifer? That was grounds for having Mother Nature pay a visit and imprison me with vines while some carnivorous plant ate me.

"Are you sure about that?" It seemed strange to hear Lucifer actually worried about something, as if he had...feelings.

Nauseatingly cute. And it in no way diminished

his cruelty to the arriving souls who deserved Perdition, the newest prison they'd just finished building in Hell. It contained the latest in torture, including a room that played the *Baby Shark* song over and over.

Shudder.

"Mother Nature is not cheating on you because she's too busy trying to protect you."

"I see."

I waited for him to rant that she was trying to emasculate him in front of his legions. He said nothing. Didn't break into dance or song either. Which was truly a blessing. He'd done that to a celebrating coven a few All Hallows' Eves ago. One never forgot the way he hit those notes in all the wrong ways and made even the most robust witches cry. And as for the dancing... He'd gotten naked and sexually scarred more than a few with his bouncing, hairy...

"You're not mad she's coddling you?" I asked, surely tugging on his horns, but I didn't understand his lack of explosion.

"That would be a waste of time. What is she protecting me from?" The words emerged low, and to my surprise, a towel suddenly appeared tucked around my head and a robe on my body.

I stepped out to find my bathroom suddenly much larger than it should be. The devil paced in the expanded space.

He muttered, too. "Gaia needs Shax to find something. But he's not in his library. He's not hiking some mountain or trekking across a wasteland. He's here on this boat, so the thing they need is here."

"Not necessarily. Shax is on this cruise because of his nephew," I reminded Lucifer.

The devil waved a hand. "Secondary. My wife is involved. She would have provided a good cover. She wanted him on this ship going..." Lucifer snapped his fingers. "To the same place we had a spy from. Ding. Ding. Ding."

"Seems kind of obvious."

Lucifer glared. "I was waiting for you to come to that conclusion. Now that you have, it's clear you need to go to Atlantis."

"In case you hadn't noticed, I am. We dock tomorrow."

"Tomorrow is too long. You must get there before Shax. Find whatever it is they seek first."

"But that would mean betraying him."

"And?" Lucifer really didn't grasp the problem with it.

"I can't."

The devil exhaled hotly. "Why the fuck not? Do you have a problem with winning?"

"No, but I do have a problem with cheating. The only reason I'm spying on Shax is because of you, which means swooping in and stealing whatever he's looking for wouldn't be right." It felt important to not screw Shax over. A perverse honor among demons and witches and all that.

The devil clearly felt differently. His eyes glowed. "Are you refusing to do your job?"

I'd have to tread carefully. "Just wondering how you think I can get there early. Unless you're planning to portal me there."

Lucifer's lips turned down. "Fuckers put some kind of shield up."

"A place you can't get into. How fascinating."

"You're supposed to be on my side," Lucifer reminded. He stood still long enough for the shadows that trailed him to stop and give him shape. The massive wings at his back, the impression of size, and menace.

"I'll be on your side when you start showing some respect, starting with knocking instead of just entering. Maybe if you tried that once in a while, people wouldn't want shields that keep you out."

"Rules. So many rules. You're ruining all the fun. Making everyone miserable. Don't do this. Don't do that." The devil roared. "It's unconscionable."

"And it's only going to get worse." The current generation liked their rules to have rules. And then those had more regulations. It wouldn't be long before Hell changed its name because someone's feelings were hurt.

"I want to know what's in Atlantis," Lucifer snapped "And I want to know yesterday."

"Too bad, so sad." To use a popular turn of phrase. "Flying via broom over that much water in search of a moving island isn't happening or even feasible."

"Then find another way. Where there's one Undine, there's probably more." The shadow mist on the devil's body suddenly expanded, hiding him. When it faded, he was gone.

The bathroom felt like a coffin, and I was running late. We were in DJ's Locker, and the ship had stopped. I'd best say hi to my daughter and son-in-law before I ran off to save Shax from himself.

Rushing out on deck, I was just in time to see my granddaughter rescue her one true love, the possessor of the locket with the love spell. I'd done it again.

But that was all I got to do. Forget saying hello to my daughter and annoying her pirate husband. Suddenly, crawling over the railing, a group of fish men confronted me.

Only three. I could handle three.

"Hello, boys." I looked at the Undines with their tiny loincloths.

A pair of them gripped spears. The middle one held out a long hunk of braided seaweed. "Hands," he gurgled.

"I don't think so." I took a step back and froze as I heard a rustle of motion.

A sharp glance over my shoulder showed three more fish men flanking me. Then another group. Nine in total to form a semi-circle while I stood with my back to the bulkhead of the ship. I kind of appreciated that they took me seriously.

I held up a balled fist. The wind flowing past halted and began to form a ball.

The fellow in charge—the Undine with the seaweed—shook his head and spit. "No magic. You come."

"Where?" I asked. If he said Atlantis, then maybe I should hitch a ride and see if I could arrive before the boat. That would please the dark lord. And then I'd share whatever info I discovered with Shax, and hopefully, prevent two gods from destroying the world.

"See king."

"Well, why didn't you say so in the first place?"

He shook the seaweed at me. "Hands. Come."

Lucifer told me to get to Atlantis before everyone else. Mission accomplished.

I held out my wrists, and when he grabbed me

with a bit more force than warranted, I chided him. "No need to get rough."

Before anyone could tie me up, the most unlikely person came to my rescue. "Don't worry, Dottie. I won't let them take you!"

Before I could give Shax hell for interrupting my kidnapping, from out of nowhere, a lasso appeared, wrapped around the left fish man, and yanked him away.

I no sooner blinked than another rope came whipping, this one managing to snare a pair.

The Undines didn't so much move as fall over as if tipped. A hole in the semi-circle opened, and Shax leapt into view, already twirling another rope.

"Lassoing?" I exclaimed. "You took up lassoing after I left?"

He smiled. "Does the least amount of damage to the books when we need to rid the library of an infestation."

Hold on. Had he just implied that he was some kind of exterminator? The way he handled that rope explained the muscles I'd seen. This mature version of Shax had a killer body and some mad skills.

Two more Undines went down, but the last one bolted. I ran after the fish man, especially because he was the only one of them all to have a special pouch dangling from his belt. I could smell the power on it from here.

What did he have? A magical object of some kind? I wanted it.

The fish man vaulted over a railing, and I followed. One light touch of my hand and I had the boost needed to soar after him. A breeze rushed up and slowed my fall. I hit with a bend of my knees and a cackle—the advantages of a younger body.

I sprinted after the Atlantean operative as he weaved through the people on deck. No one paid us any mind. A Hell cruise often had people running for their lives.

I headed right to the very tip of the ship, where a heap of netting sat in an untidy pile. I thought that odd but ignored it until the soggy mound moved.

More fish men piled out, brandishing snarls and weapons. So many of them sent to capture little ol' me.

I was rather flattered.

Before I could waggle my fingers, Shax waded in. The rope he was using was now some kind of nylon thing, not as slick as the one he'd used before. But he still did some damage, especially when he went after the fish men, fists swinging. He didn't have as much raw magic as I did. He appeared to be more defensive.

My style tended to be on the more aggressive side. I balled my fist and held it out. *Come to me.* I called the magic, reached out to the sea. Born of land but a daughter of water. A sea witch, the ocean answered and filled me. I flung a ball of power that bowled a few Undines over. But more of them arrived, and I wondered that no one had sounded the alarm on the ship. No one said a thing.

As if reading my mind, Shax yelled, "They have a shield hiding us."

The moment he said it, I could see a glimmer. Someone with magic camouflaged the Undines' actions.

And still, they swarmed, cutting us off from the ship. Separating us. Meaning I could stop pretending and fighting.

A bellow sounded, that of an angry beast somewhere on the cruise liner, followed by the cannonball of all splashes. It rocked the ship. Enough to send me off balance and right into someone.

Something cold went around my neck, and I looked down.

I wore a necklace.

Of pearls.

Uh-oh.

I knew what these were. "Ursula's pearls," I muttered, clutching at the strand. The fact that they were around my neck meant this had been a targeted attack. Against me. Kind of flattering and predictable.

"I see you recognize the jewelry. Then you know what they do."

The group of Undines parted, and I glared at the man who came to stand in front of me, his helm shaped like a crown. He wore a toga over his body, the chainmail pretty but more ornamental than for protection. Square-jawed, not bad-looking. A dead man walking given what he'd done. But not yet. I had use of him still.

I sneered. "You think to stifle my magic with jewelry?"

"Not think. Have. You are under my control now. I have the crest." He held up a ring. "You will do as I say. When I say it."

"And you are?"

"The King of Atlantis. Let's go."

"Where?" My fingers rolled over the pearls. I had yet to test the boundaries of the necklace.

"My kingdom, of course. Take her."

The fish men surrounded me and wrapped me in seaweed tight enough that I could barely breathe. But I wasn't worried. They wanted me alive.

As they tossed me overboard into the water, I caught an angry gaze. Not yet bound, Shax watched from amidst the Undines, who didn't pay him enough mind.

I mouthed, "*See you in Atlantis.*"

His eyes widened, and then I only saw the side of the ship as I plummeted to the ocean.

7

SHAX: DOES SHE WANT ME TO SAVE HER? SHOULD I SAVE HER? ALL THE BOOKS CONTRADICT THEMSELVES.

WHEN THOSE FISH men tossed Dottie off the ship, I saw the smirk on her face. She was going with them on purpose to beat me to Atlantis. She knew I was on a quest for Mother Nature and fucked me over anyhow.

Because she put Lucifer's orders ahead of me.

I had to beat her there. Turning to the nearest fish man, I dropped the rope I'd yanked free from the waistband of my swim shorts. More garrote than lasso, but it would work.

"Look, I'm surrendering. Take me to your city." I even held out my hands.

There was something immensely irritating about the wave of fish men ignoring me and leaving the ship. Diving off the side, disappearing with Dottie, abandoning me with no way to follow.

"Argh!" I bellowed. I stomped back to my quarters to see myself standing in the hall.

I blinked. "Uh, excuse me. Who the hell are you?"

The image of me wavered, and Gaia appeared. She waved. "Hi."

No explanation for why she wore my body.

"What were you doing? Why were you being me?"

"Because you couldn't exactly be in two places at once, of course, silly." She rolled her eyes.

"You're right, I couldn't. So, what was I doing here?" I pointed to the door to Ian's room where she stood.

"I was being supportive, seeing as how you were busy."

"Why did Ian need support?" I shoved past Mother Nature and scanned the room. The *empty* room. "Where is he?"

"A trio of Undines kind of stole his wife, and he went completely kraken. Last I saw, he was chasing after her. Super romantic if you ask me."

I took a moment to process what Gaia had just said. "Some fish men took Sasha?"

Mother Nature nodded.

"And you did nothing to stop them?"

Gaia shrugged. "It would have ruined my disguise."

"You let them take my nephew's wife, the only thing that could cure him, and now he's gone, too. Fuck me!" I yelled, scrubbing at my face. I stomped through Ian's room and went right to the railing. I saw nothing. He'd be long gone. Just like Dorothy was.

I'd failed them both. I whirled and stomped back into the suite, pointing a finger. "You need to help me get to Atlantis."

"I told you, I can't."

"Then how am I supposed to get there?"

"The ship docks in the morning."

The mightiness of my glare did not shrivel Gaia's expression in the least. "Tomorrow might be too late."

"Sorry, but in this place, my powers are too limited."

I sighed. "Do me a favor then, please. In the future, if you're not going to save people I care about, don't pretend to be me."

"Then how would you have had that lovely chat with Ian?"

"What chat? Argh. Never mind. Go away." Yes, I yelled at a goddess. I didn't particularly care.

She did. She sniffed. "Be that way. I'll go where I'm wanted." With a burst of petals, she disappeared.

"I hear they're looking for space cadets," I

muttered. I paced, sorting through my options, of which there were few.

I couldn't hope to follow the fish men under water. With night falling, even if I could manage a boat, I'd never be able to track their trail.

But the *Sushi Lover* wouldn't dock at Atlantis until the morning. Too long. Surely, there was another way.

I bellowed for Lucifer.

He apparated, looking bleary-eyed, his son sleeping wrapped around his neck, the dark lord's robe appearing as if it had gone through a war with baby spit-up. "This better be good," he shout-whispered. "This is our nap time."

"The Atlantean king kidnapped Dorothy, and I think he took Ian's wife, too."

"Excellent."

"How is that excellent?"

The devil blew a raspberry. "Because they're agents of chaos. Where they go, interesting things follow."

My lips pressed tight. "Aren't you the least bit concerned? Dottie is your minion."

"Who can handle herself without my help. I wouldn't dare offer." Lucifer shook his head.

"I'd usually agree, but I don't know if she can

defend herself. They put some kind of pearl necklace on her."

"Really? I didn't take her for the kinky type." Lucifer's gaze brightened.

I snapped. "Not that kind of necklace. A real one. With giant pearls."

"Still kinky. You obviously don't know how they're made. Neptune has a fine gig going with those suckers. Mine is only fit to burn." The devil glanced down at his groin with a moue of annoyance.

"What does the necklace do?" I asked since the devil had veered off track.

"Those are known as Ursula's pearls. The strand was specially made eons ago to control sea witches. It stifles their power. Makes them malleable to the commands of the one who controls the matching ring."

"Oh, Dottie won't like that," I muttered.

"I daresay it's the king who won't like the result. Thinking he can pearl a witch of mine. I shall have to ensure a good seat to watch on the morrow. The showdown will be delicious."

"Or you could help me get to the island early, perform some daring rescue in your name, and show this king he shouldn't mess with minions serving Hell." My words got a little loud at the end.

The baby stirred.

Lucifer froze. I held my breath.

"Gngngn." The baby continued to snore.

Lucifer relaxed and said in a hushed tone, "I will not indulge your patriarchal fantasy of riding to a little woman's rescue."

I blinked at him. "What the fuck did you just say?"

A grin pulled at the devil's lips. "Just quoting some of the new shit coming out of my lawyer's office. Part of the non-bias based on everything rule. I'm thinking of incorporating it more widely. I mean, there's so many applications for it. Think of the number of potential hero types we could decimate by recognizing that everyone is strong and can save themselves."

"Sometimes, people need to be rescued." In Dottie's case, it had nothing to do with her strength or her abilities. The right thing to do involved action, not standing by and watching.

The baby grumbled and squirmed. Lucifer glared at me and mouthed, *"You are dead if he wakes."*

The baby settled, and I was the one to breathe in relief.

"Are you sure this isn't sour grapes that Dorothy is apparently doing a better job of sussing out interesting things than you are? She makes a much better minion," Lucifer declared.

"I thought Dorothy being kidnapped by the king of Atlantis was interesting."

"Not really. King Rex." The devil sneered. "He thinks he's such a big shot. Have you seen the size of his cock? The term baby finger comes to mind."

I winced. "Ouch." But reassuring. Dorothy would probably laugh if he came after her with his teenie winkie. "Why would he go through so much trouble to steal a sea witch?"

"Why does anyone want them? Disagreeable lot. They have potty mouths. Attitude. And tempers. Is it any wonder they're among my favorites?" Lucifer muttered, his expression soft with fondness.

"I'm pretty sure the king didn't steal Dorothy for her cussing abilities."

"No, more like her spell-making ones. She is the most proficient sea witch currently alive. Even her sister can't hold a candle to her."

"Rex thinks he can use her." Again, something Dottie wouldn't like.

"The man—fish?—has been living on the bottom of the ocean too long. He really hasn't the slightest clue how things work. I blame the inbreeding. Your mother shouldn't also be your sister and your aunt. His great-grandfather really couldn't keep track."

Off topic again, I reeled Lucifer back. "Are you or are you not going to help me? Because if you're just going to run your mouth, then you can leave." Frustration over Dottie had me lashing out at the devil. And I really didn't care.

The baby opened a sleepy lid and peeked at me.

The devil didn't notice, and the baby closed his eye again.

"Chill out, dude." Lucifer did a horrible impression of a surfer dude, and the baby burp-smiled in its sleep. The devil gazed at him with something akin to affection. "Such a pity everything keeps saying he has to die."

I blinked. "You're planning to kill your son?"

"Not yet. There's no challenge when they're this small. But in a few decades, when he comes after me, I won't have a choice."

"What makes you think he will?"

Lucifer softly quoted. "'For the child shall inherit the kingdom of the father, sit upon the throne, and wear the crown of fire and thorns. But it shan't be a gentle passing, and the blood of the mother shall stain the hands of the child, soaking into the very river of death to signal the start of a new reign.'"

I blinked. "That's—"

"The prophecy my wife has been searching for.

The one that disappeared from Hell's library a while back."

"You have it?"

Lucifer rolled his shoulders, and the baby did a chubby-armed stretch, still sleeping, but his mouth opened to yawn. "I used to have it. I threw it in Hell's furnace when I found out that Gaia was pregnant."

"Why?" I whispered the word. Because I didn't get the impression that fear had led to him destroying a prophecy.

Lucifer eyed me. The baby opened a sleepy lid and watched me. In an uncanny moment of synchronicity, they both smiled, mirror images of evil. It was Lucifer who said, "Because it is the only one that claims Gaia will die, too."

I had a moment of stunned silence as my mind wrapped around the admission. "You don't want Gaia to have it because it involves her."

"It involves her being killed by our child!" Lucifer growled. "The one thing she loves almost as much as me. It has to be a lie. I won't let it happen."

It was strangely romantic in a perverse way.

"So, you would prevent my possible death but do nothing about your own?" Gaia appeared in a swirl of green taffeta.

Lucifer drew up tall. Taller surely than the ceiling had room for. "I am the Lord of Hell. I am allowed to be selfish. I insist all the prophecies be about me. And only me."

"Those damned things all claim you die by our son's hand. I won't allow it."

"He is the Son of Perdition. The Branch of the Terrible Ones," Lucifer intoned. "He won't have a choice."

"We all have a choice, you big, horny idiot." Gaia somehow managed to be in Lucifer's arms, the fabric of her skirt swirling around his legs.

"We do get to choose, and mine involves ensuring you have a long life. So, deal with it," the devil growled.

"Oh, Luc." She breathed his name as she gave him a kiss.

I stared at the ceiling, ignoring the wet sounds that followed. The baby wisely made a noise of complaint.

"How did you know I was looking for the prophecy?" Gaia asked, a touch breathless.

"Ah, my dear, conniving wife. Did you really think I wouldn't know you were visiting another man?" Lucifer's nose flared, and his breath huffed hot smoke.

"Jealous?" she said, batting lashes that resembled the wings of a butterfly.

"Extremely. When was the last time you snuck

off to be with me?"

"Is my big, bad devil feeling neglected?"

"Yes."

I began to inch away as the passion between them charged, two forces of nature, pushing and pulling, ready to combust.

With a baby between them.

Lucifer and Gaia stared at each other.

"I need you," he said.

"Need you more," she parroted. "Shax, be a dear and mind Damian for us."

"But—Dottie—and Ian—and—"

"Everything will be fine. You'll see Dorothy tomorrow when we dock in Atlantis. Ian is screwed no matter what. So, enjoy some time with Damian. After all, you are his demon father." The non-Catholic equivalent of a Godfather.

I groaned. "Why me?"

"Because I lost a coin toss," Lucifer grumbled. "Now, stop being a cock-blocker and take the baby."

Before I could run screaming, the baby ended up on my shoulder, snoring and drooling.

Gaia waggled her fingers. "We'll grab him in the morning before we dock. Remember, he only drinks breastmilk."

Plink. Plink.

A pair of bottles appeared alongside a stack of diapers and sleepers.

"But…"

"I owe you," Lucifer said with a wink. "Now, I'm off to plow me wench."

"Oh, I'll shiver your timbers, all right." A giggle that faded as they stepped through a portal to somewhere else, leaving me with the devil's baby.

Since I'd only cared for Ian starting at the toddler years, I had no issue at all hunting down a true expert. Valaska took pity on me and let me hang out with her family. When the baby woke, my nieces/nephews kept the child entertained. Then Damian kept us busy for a few hours, chasing after him as he pulled a baby Jack and kept popping in and out of places on the ship. Inside the mouth of an Orc proved to be the most heart-stopping place.

By dawn, we were all passed out, me on the floor with Damian tied to my chest.

"Rise and shine, mateys!" It was a beaming Lucifer who came to fetch the child as the ship docked.

I groaned. The baby stretched, the rope just falling through his body. Freed, Damian extended his pudgy arms. "Da!"

"There's my boy! Did you drive them absolutely crazy?" Lucifer chuckled as he bent to grab him.

From this angle, the hickey on the devil's neck was bright green.

The baby clung to his father with a giggle.

"The kid actually likes you," I said almost in surprise.

"For now. Eventually, I always let them down." Lucifer's expression almost appeared sad as he glanced down at his son, who snuggled against the devil's chest.

"Your daughter Muriel still likes you, and Bambi's pretty close, too."

"For now. Muriel is only coming into her power. And if she turned against me, Bambi would follow. Even my own granddaughter could pose a dilemma one day."

"Yet you let them live," I remarked.

"It was time to stop killing them in the womb," Lucifer said with a shrug. "Even the original devil can't rule forever."

A strange thing for him to say.

"Any word on Dorothy and what the king has done with her?"

"Really, Shax. Asking me to do your job for you. I don't know how you expect me to have had time in between debauching my wife and defiling the mother of my child to look into the mere kidnapping of one of my witches." Lucifer began to fade

133

from sight, but I heard one last thing. "A word of advice. The prophecy is no longer in the library. And neither is a cure for Ian. So, don't waste your time looking."

Truth or a lie? With the devil, you could never know for sure.

Relieved of my babysitting chore, I managed to make it ashore before the rest of the passengers. Easy enough to clamber down a tethering rope and find my way onto the docks. No one saw me. I had the Forgotten Book in my pocket, a tiny tome often overlooked, its ability to remain hidden in plain sight growing as it aged. Even better, a person holding such a magical thing might be ignored, as well.

I had many useful books packed in a bag. I never left the library without an arsenal. The saying that the word was mightier than the sword? Sometimes, it was true, if you had the right tome. And I had access to the best.

As the dawn rose, lighting the delicate coral stone minarets of Atlantis, I made my way through shadowed streets to the palace. I knew the path, having studied the city before even coming on this trip.

My guess was that Dorothy and Ian's wife would either be close to the king or in the dungeons under the castle. As for Ian... A glance over my shoulder, and I saw him heading in his man shape for the palace, as well. According to Adexios, he'd returned to the ship in the early hours of the morning—without his wife.

I thought of slowing down and waiting for him, but every second might count. Ian could handle himself. I had my own mission.

Library or throne room? I'd yet to make the decision which to hit first. Lucifer had told me not to bother with the library, which made me think I should. After all, it was part of my original plan.

Before reaching the final steps leading to the palace, I pulled out the Forgotten Book and promptly had no idea what was going on.

Look, there're some stairs. Should I go up them? Are those guards? I don't see any. They don't see me. Let's just go past them.

I almost forgot to put the book back into my pocket. Once I did, though, it reduced some of the book's effect. Blinking, I had to reorient myself and move quickly. Someone might notice the very demon-looking fellow wandering the halls.

When I heard a noise, I put my hand on the book. I only made two wrong turns before finding the library. A massive space, it tunneled down several stories. I could see the many rings as it descended, tiers of shelves. Empty shelves.

Impossible.

I found a ladder and climbed down to see the shelves practically bare. Only in the lower levels did I find a few stone tablets along with someone cleaning.

The fish man didn't even look up as I approached. "You there, mopping the floor, where are the books?" Had they been stored elsewhere?

"No books." The words burbled from the heavily fishy male in his loincloth with his rag and bucket.

"What do you mean, no books? This is a library. The library of Atlantis. It's famous for its knowledge."

"No more. Gone. Sank." The fish man exploded his hands. "Books melt. All gone."

I stared at the shelves in disbelief.

I'd come here for nothing. I'd made the wrong choice. I glanced up and steeled myself for the climb.

The janitor gurgled. "Faster." He pointed a gray-scaled hand that was more fin.

I noticed a glass tower in the corner tucked into the wall itself so only the front of it showed, the water inside agitated. There was a circle in front of it.

I stood on it and said, "How does it—glurg." It sucked me into the watery tube, and I shot up, up, up.

Out!

I flailed my arms and legs as the water cannon shot me out a hole. I had a second to notice the surprised face of a guard before slamming into him.

I lifted myself muttering, "Sorry about that. Your elevator system needs to come with a warning."

The guard groaned and didn't get up. Probably for the best.

I limped off the impact as I traced my way to the throne room. The Forgotten Book helped me past some more guards, allowing me to ease into a kickass throne room.

Tall pillars reached to an open sky. A fountain in the center spewed water. A dais with a big-ass chair, a king sitting on it.

My Dottie looked like an annoyed statue standing beside the throne, and Ian, my poor nephew, was dodging spears.

Too many of them. The boy did his best to weave, but sheer volume felled him, and I was too far away.

A spear struck him in the thigh, and Ian dropped to a knee.

The boy I'd raised. The one I'd learned to make cakes for. Who'd taught me the worst knock-knock jokes. Who loved me. He was going to die in front of me. I could already see the next round of spears aiming, readying to fly.

My gaze went to Dorothy, silently begging even as I ran to try and stop it.

Those damned pearls remained around her neck. She wouldn't be able to act.

"Ian, no," I huffed, sprinting for him, seeing the arc as all those pointed missiles sailed towards my nephew.

I stumbled in disbelief as they all clattered to the floor, broken and bent as if they'd hit a shield.

A smile spread across my face as Dottie turned to the king by her side, her lips pulled back over her teeth. "How dare you?"

The king rose and began to back away. "Impossible. You wear the necklace. You must obey."

Relief made me chuckle as I neared the dais. "You obviously don't know Dottie very well. She doesn't take orders—"

"—from anyone!" she snapped. She wrapped her fingers around the necklace and yanked, tugging until it broke, and the pearls scattered, the only noise in the silence that fell. They bounced off the dais and plinked down the steps before rolling to a stop all over the floor.

A breeze arose out of nowhere, hot and hinting of ozone. Overhead, dark clouds formed, hiding the warm sun, and the wind turned sharper, colder, slapping into the warm breeze, a clash that had lightning flashing, immediately followed by a thundering boom.

Dorothy's hair whipped as she hissed, "How dare you think to control a sea witch? I am mightier than any king."

Also more beautiful than anything I'd ever seen. Powerful, too, with magic at her command. I almost applauded when she pointed at the stunned king. He barely had time to yell before he got slapped with a hard burst of wind. It propelled him off his feet into a pillar.

He landed with a thump and cracked the totem. Both fell to the floor.

I glanced away from Dorothy to Ian. He yanked the spear out of his leg, and I winced in sympathy.

My fault. I should have come straight here and ignored the library.

Those fighting noticed me, and even the Forgotten Book couldn't make them all *un*see my presence. Fish men poured in and attacked. While Dottie handled some, I had to take care of others. A wild and wet battle broke out, with the wind whipping raindrops against my skin. Lightning illuminated the makeshift battle ring in a burst that blinded. Thunder rattled the very air all around and stunned the ears.

For every creature I brought down, another took

its place. A glance showed Ian on his feet, barely, leaning on a broken spear as a crutch. Dorothy did better, still toying with the king, smashing him into pillars while holding off his guards. But she couldn't do this forever. I could already see the use of all that magic taxing her strength. We needed out of here.

Even more soldiers poured into the throne room, rushing for Dottie, the biggest threat. She didn't let it daunt her but flung bursts of wind that tossed the soldiers around. With a cackle, she jabbed her finger to strike with lightning.

Whereas all I had in my back pocket was a tiny, unknown book titled *Eat my Cape*, a superhero fan fiction that had some power because the writer had poured their life force into it. While the author's death never made them famous, it allowed me to use some magic, but it was erratic. At times, when I pointed and channeled my ability, squids shot out of nowhere to splat on the faces of soldiers. Other times, they exploded and covered everything in slick goo. And then Dorothy's power failed.

"It's fizzling!" she screeched. She waggled her fingers, trying to ignite her power, only getting a weak zap. She'd mentioned needing to recharge because of some big love spell. It meant that we were done fighting.

But soldiers kept moving in.

"Conserve what you have left." It was the only advice I could think of, while my mind whirled for how I could help.

The fish men sensed her weakness and moved as if to swarm. I shoved my hand into one last pocket and withdrew my palm-sized *Book of Water*. Containing aquatically-inclined poems written by a mad warlock, it did the most interesting things. I aimed it at the strongest water source in the room. The fountain. The liquid in it churned and rose, flooding through the air, blasting the soldiers to the ground. It allowed my nephew to hobble close to Dottie and me, and once he got within range, the water formed a liquid shield around us.

"How long can you hold it?" Dottie asked.

"Not long. We need out of here, pronto. Do you have enough magic to fly?"

"Only if you can pull a broom out of your ass," she retorted.

Good thing I'd learned how to improvise. "How's a spear?" I swept a shaft from the ground and offered it to her.

"You do realize my magic is just about tapped out, right?"

"We just need enough to make it to the ship. Once there, Adexios will protect us. He won't let anyone hurt his favorite uncle." I grinned, offering some attempt at reassurance.

Ian still bled and looked none too steady on his feet. And if Dorothy couldn't use magic, then we wouldn't last long.

Dorothy slid the shaft between her legs. "It's crazy enough that it might just work. We'll have to huddle close to make sure we all fit. And be warned, we might get wet." She gave me a coy peek over her shoulder.

She expected me to refuse. I'd lived long enough to not give a shit about appearances. I sat bitch behind her, but Ian balked.

I beckoned him to come closer. "Hold on tight to me, Ian, this could be bumpy."

I wasn't surprised to see Ian shake his head. I'd expected it, especially since I could see the beast within pulsing under his skin.

"I'll take my chances on land. Go." He waved at us. "I need to find Sasha."

"But the guards..." I glanced at my shield and the bodies behind it. Saw the determination on Ian's face. The book in my hand was almost tapped out. But it could do one more thing. "I love you, Ian."

He nodded, and I knew in that moment that this was the last time we'd speak. The monster was coming, and I couldn't stop it. But I could at least give Ian a chance to reach the water.

I thrust my arms out, channeling all the magic left in the book even as I knew it would destroy it. Giving it a burst of power exploded my watery shield, knocking down the soldiers, and giving Ian a bubble to move.

Dottie murmured, "We have to go. Now."

Barely enough warning for me to grab hold of her as the spear lifted. Jostled. I lost sight of Ian for a moment, and when I did glimpse him again, another spear hung from him.

"No," I muttered, only to watch wide-eyed as Dorothy circled, showing the transformation of man to beast.

The rain turned Ian's skin slick, not mottled as you'd expect, but a steel gray with hints of blue and green. And he was massive. The size of my nephew, the boy I thought of as a son, engulfed the throne room, knocked down more pillars, and caused a rumble that had Dottie pulling up.

"We need to move away from the disturbance," she muttered, angling away.

Holding her around the waist, I could only watch. "Ian's turned kraken."

I pointed, for sure enough, my nephew clambered down the sheer cliff upon which the castle resided, using his tentacles to move down and then smash his way inside.

"What's he doing?"

For a moment, I wasn't sure. Why hadn't Ian climbed down to the ocean?

Then I saw it. The king running down a street. Slithering fast behind, the kraken.

Given the island was sinking, guess who won?

The king got smashed into a building, Ian slipped down a sewer, squeezing his massive bulk in somehow. On his way to find Sasha, and quickly, before Atlantis sank entirely.

The ocean churned around the shores, a frothing, violent sway of water. Screams filled the air as the ship's passengers who'd eagerly filed off the cruise liner came stampeding back.

But I watched the city. Ian was in there. "I have to help him."

"You can't breathe water," was Dorothy's reply.

I pursed my lips. "I can't do nothing."

"You can't help if you drown either. We have to land. I can't keep us aloft anymore," she hissed as her magic fizzled.

She aimed for the ship, and the landing proved a little bumpy as we sprawled on the deck with my face in her bosom. Not the worst place to be, I could admit.

But I didn't have time to enjoy it. Leaping to my feet, I ran for the rail and shoved through the passengers milling and murmuring. I had to see what had happened. I cursed the moment I did. The first level of Atlantis was already submerged. Water streamed down the streets, and I saw no sign of my nephew.

"Where is he?" I muttered. I scanned the waters, noticing more than a few rescue boats from the ship being launched to pick up those who'd not run fast enough. No giant kraken came to overturn them.

"Look to your left," Dorothy yelled.

I whirled and saw the water agitating. A giant form floated to the surface, tentacle outstretched, holding…a body.

"He found Sasha!" I yelled.

I wasn't the only one who noticed Ian's return. A giant harpoon went flying and narrowly missed the kraken. The city fought back.

I could see more harpoonists lining up.

"No. No." I could only watch as several of the large missiles hit my nephew, striking him hard. He began to sink, taking his wife with him.

"That's not good," Dottie mumbled.

I could only stare at the water and heave a sigh of relief when an appendage broke the surface to fling a body to safety. A short-lived relief.

The tentacle disappeared.

"Ian?" The name trembled on my lips.

The water went still.

Too still.

"Ian." I couldn't help the aching loss. I sank to my knees. He was gone. The boy I loved more than anything.

Gone.

Dorothy put her arm around me. "Come."

"But...Ian." I'd failed him. My shoulders slumped.

"You can't do anything for him right now."

We returned to my room, the grief weighing me down. For a moment, I contemplated screaming at the unfairness. Instead, I got mad at Dorothy.

"You betrayed me!"

8

DOROTHY: NOTHING MORE DANGEROUS THAN SOMEONE WHO IS HURTING.

THE ANGUISH in Shax broke him. He cried. The loss of his nephew shook him to the core. And he needed someone to blame.

"How did I betray you? I was kidnapped. My magic controlled by that pearl necklace."

Shax snorted. "You allowed them to take you. Instead of waiting, facing it together, you betrayed me. And now, Ian is gone."

"I tried to save him." A weak reply to a man who'd lost someone he considered a son.

"I want to be alone." The demand emerged so coldly.

"Shax." I went to touch him, but he moved out of my reach, no more the flirting man.

"Not right now. I can't." He hung his head. "I should have been there for him. Instead, I allowed myself to get caught up in you. And for nothing. Stupid me, I thought you were starting to care."

"I am. I do."

"You chose the dark lord over me."

"It wasn't like that."

"Wasn't it?" he snapped, and I knew it was because he hurt, but the verbal lashing still stung with the truth. "You intentionally let the fish men take you."

"Yes, but—"

"No buts. You did it so you could beat me to the prophecy."

"I would have shared it with you."

"No, you wouldn't have, because Lucifer wanted you to find it so it could be destroyed."

"Only I didn't give it to him," I huffed quickly.

"Because it doesn't exist. You betrayed me for nothing. I saw the library." His lips turned down. "I thought I could find something to save Ian in there. I should have known that books would fail me again."

"What's that supposed to mean?"

"A long time ago, you accused me of loving my library more than you. You were right and wrong. I loved it, but I would have burned it down in a heartbeat if I could have had you. Yet, you left me. Just dropped me cold. And it broke something in me. But

I learned to get past that, to heal." He eyed me. "And now, I'm broken again."

The ache in my chest tightened my throat. "Shax." I cupped his cheeks, but he wouldn't look at me.

"Don't. I can't. Not after what I did to Ian."

"You didn't do anything."

"Didn't I?" He met my gaze with eyes blazing. "I chose you over my own damned nephew. And look how that turned out. He's dead."

"Don't be so sure. Look outside."

Shax turned, and for a moment, he said nothing. Then he ran to the rail and hugged the tentacle that rose ridiculously high from the water. The size of the sea monster boggled the mind.

"He's not dead," he said, turning watery eyes on me. "But he can't come back."

The tentacle slid back under the waves.

"I thought his birthday was tomorrow."

"Hell runs almost twelve hours early compared to this time zone." His lips turned down. "It's his birthday."

I put my hand on his shoulder. "I'm sorry."

"If you don't mind, I'd like to be alone."

A part of me screamed that I should stay. Remain and support him. Another part of me demanded that I act. Entering the hall, I looked for a good spot. The utility room at the far end gave me the privacy needed.

I entered the closet and hissed, "Lucifer!"

"Oooh, demanding a rendezvous in a secluded place. Maybe I can tell Gaia I didn't know it was you in the dark."

"Stop flirting. You need to help Shax."

"I'm pretty sure Gaia's no-cheating rule applies to him, too."

"Not that kind of help." I rolled my eyes. "Ian. You have to do something about Ian."

"Me? Whatever for?"

"Because he works for you."

"Shax was working for Gaia first. Maybe he should ask her for a favor since they're so close." The reply emerged snottily.

"Argh. You can be such a child. What is it going to take to get you to help?"

"I'm partial to begging. Knees. Bent over. I'm not picky how you plead." Lucifer leered, his expression lit like a demonic candle inside a pumpkin coming alive on All Hallows' Eve once it turned dark.

"Don't start that shit. Help the boy."

"Where's the information you were supposed to get?"

"There is nothing to report. The library was

destroyed when Atlantis sank. Shax walked away empty-handed."

"That's unfortunate. And insufficient to bargain for Ian's life. Now, if you don't mind, I'm being paged." Lucifer cocked his head. A hint of brimstone and he disappeared.

No sooner did the scorching sensation subside than I found my nose tickling with the scent of flowers.

Gaia appeared in a fluff of daffodils that fluttered before settling into a gown. "I thought he'd never leave. Show me. I know you have it."

I clamped my lips. "Excuse me?"

It was as if a light had flicked on. A tiny army of glow bugs lit the room, which was lined with shelves and cleaning supplies.

Gaia gazed at me with eyes that reflected green. "I'm talking about the prophecy, of course. I noticed you didn't hand it over to my husband."

"Because there's nothing to hand over. The library was destroyed by the ocean. Nothing but empty shelves now."

Gaia's lips pursed. "Well, that's inconvenient."

"Not really. I'd say Ian got the worst of it. And Shax is really hurting."

A flick of Gaia's hand and a shake of her head loosened a few small bugs that caused a whir of sound as their wings beat to keep them aloft. "Oh, the drama. I can see what Lucifer means. So annoying that no one ever listens. I told Shax everything would turn out all right. He should have faith."

"How can everything be all right when his nephew is a permanent sea monster?"

"Not anymore, he isn't." Gaia's smile turned sly. "A deal was brokered, a curse undone."

"What?" I blinked.

"See for yourself."

Gaia snapped her fingers, and it was as if I had a window to the outside. I saw Shax still leaning on the railing, despondent. Then he straightened. His eyes widened. He scrambled to toss a life ring, and the angle of the vision changed to show me a body floating on the surface of the water.

Ian had returned.

"Thank you." A heartfelt emotion.

"Don't thank me. My most extraordinary husband is the one who came to the rescue. It would seem Sasha Farseer is wilier than I gave her credit for. She struck a bargain with Luc. Handy things, those contracts. I need to start having a few of my own. Perhaps I'll start with the Farseer girl. Seek her out for a new prophecy." Gaia smiled at me and twiddled her fingers. "Buh-bye."

Gaia disappeared in a shower of pollen that clung

to me and snowed on the floor of the hallway when I stepped out. To make matters worse, it glittered, leaving a shower of sparkles in my wake. I ran to Shax's door and pounded.

He opened it, wild-haired and crazy-eyed. "He's all right!"

"I know!" I took a quick peek around for candles lest I accidentally burn down another room. And then I kissed him.

A kiss that resulted in me being dragged into his room. The door kicked shut.

He walked me to the bed.

"What." Lip suck. "About." Hot slant. "Ian?"

He murmured the reply, never losing contact with my mouth. "He is celebrating with his wife."

"Are we celebrating, too?"

Shax paused for a moment, looking down at me, so intent I forgot to breathe.

"I've wanted to finish our first kiss for centuries. I really don't care if the ship sinks. The world ends. Or if I die for doing this. I need to be with you."

"You had me at finish our first kiss." I stroked his cheek. "I'm happy I found you again."

His mouth crushed mine, a torrid embrace that saw us tumbling to the bed, him on the bottom, me in control on top.

I wasn't a virgin. I knew my way around a man's

body, and yet being with Shax proved different. I found myself experiencing a strange breathlessness. Every tug on my lower lip, a jolt to my sex. Every stroke of his hand on my body ignited my every last nerve.

His tongue slid along mine, the most intimate thing we could do with our mouths. Except for one other...

I let my lips slide along his jaw, rubbing against it. When he growled and made as if he'd roll us, I pushed him down, a little magic to hold him.

He went still. "So that's how it's going to be?"

I grinned down at him and winked. "You've been fantasizing all this time. Let's see if I can live up to it."

There was nothing more gratifying than having a man swallow hard, his cock straining, waiting for me to release it.

It took only a little bit of magic to unmake all the stitching on his clothes. The garments slid from Shax easily after that as I stroked my hands over him. Revealing skin. Places to kiss. I touched, and he trembled. Groaned a few times, too.

I liked it when he did that. So, I kissed his body some more, fascinated by the lean lines of his physique. Intrigued by the scars of a man who'd done battle.

He gasped as I kissed my way past his navel, my hands tugging the loose fabric that used to be his pants and underwear.

"Dottie!"

He ended my name on a high note as I grabbed him. Firmly. He throbbed a bit in my grasp.

I kept him in my hand while I watched his face. Such an expressive mien.

He looked as if he were in pain.

The kind of agony that had to do with need.

He needed me. I blew on him.

The lovely shudder he gifted me... I blew again and licked. Ran my tongue over his swollen head. Tasted him. Watched him as I pleasured him. It ignited my desire to see him writhe at my mercy.

I sucked him, and his hips bucked. He groaned, breath heavy, even hummed as I teased him, sucking hard a few times before stopping when I felt him get tense.

"Come here," he growled. His eyes glowed. His body gleamed.

"Why?" I teased, blowing the words around his cock.

"Because it's my turn."

I could have fought him, remained in control, but I chose to let him flip me to my back. My clothes didn't need magic for him to remove. His sharp tugs ripped me bare. He straddled me, the tip of him jutting as he stared at my body.

Not that of the young girl he once knew.

He devoured me hungrily with his eyes. Then his lips.

He didn't start at the top, he went for the dip of my belly. His face pressed against the soft skin. The hint of stubble rubbing at my flesh.

It was my turn to gasp as he kissed his way lower, hot, sliding kisses to my thighs, bringing a subtle tremble to them. Then a short cry as he touched my core. He parted my nether lips with a tongue and found me ready for him.

He hummed his appreciation against me as he lapped. Each firm lick of his tongue heightened my pleasure, increased my need.

Until I moaned his name. "Shax." I held out my arms for him, and he came for me.

His lips found mine, the taste of me on them. He kissed me as the head of his shaft found the softness between my legs.

He pushed in as I grabbed his shoulders and dug in my nails. My head fell back, and my lips parted as he sheathed himself in me. Long and thick. Just the way I wanted him.

As he began to move inside me, I clung to him,

loving the weight of him, the sheer maleness. "I love you," I whispered against the pulse in his neck.

He found my mouth for a torrid kiss as he thrust into me, finding that sweet spot inside. He hit it. Over and over. Could he feel how tight I'd gotten around him?

Because I could sure feel how he pulsed inside me. And when he came?

The hard spasm caused me to ripple, as well. My orgasm hit. Intense and bright. A perfect moment of joining.

And someone just had to ruin it.

9

SHAX: NO BOOK CAN COMPARE TO REAL LIFE.

"HA, I found you a love match. I knew he was perfect for you. Booyah!" Lucifer fist-pumped at the foot of the bed, earning a glare from me.

Dottie flung an arm over her eyes and groaned. "I will never hear the end of this."

"End of what? The fact that I'm always right? And I know how to matchmake? Who's better than that little fucker Cupid? Me. That's right." Lucifer did a little dance, and I hid my eyes.

The audience got bigger as Gaia appeared. "Really, Luc? Must you gloat?"

"Fucking right, I need to gloat," gloated the devil. "The bet was if I won, you'd make me a sandwich."

That made me remove my arm from my face. "Why do you want her to make you a sandwich? You have a cook."

"She knows why." Lucifer winked at Gaia.

Mother Nature tittered so hard, a shower of ladybugs shook out of her gown. The odd lump on the front of her moved. A baby's face peeked out of the fabric draped over her torso.

"Ma?"

Gaia's face softened as she glanced at the baby. "We might have to wait until later. The nannies are all still recovering."

"Nef is available!" Lucifer offered with a wide grin.

Mother Nature narrowed her gaze on Dottie and me. "Why bother that old sorceress when we have two perfectly suitable babysitters right here. They don't mind, I'm sure." Gaia's smile was pure evil.

The devil had never looked hornier.

And I'd never wanted to cry more than when a baby landed on the bed between my witch and me.

"See you in a few hours. Maybe." Lucifer curled his arm around his wife, and they were gone.

Dottie eyed me over the child's head and mouthed, "I love you."

I kind of wanted to jump off the ship to cool my ardor, but I winked. "I love you, too. Wanna help me teach the baby to hogtie his daddy?"

One never knew when that might come in handy. After all, the kid was the Son of Perdition.

The following day as we packed and prepared to depart, Dottie rummaged in her purse, armpit deep, mumbling, "I know it's in here somewhere."

She pulled out a wallet. A tiny thing barely large enough for a credit card. "I found it."

"Found what?"

"My passport. Didn't you say something about traveling?" She retrieved a battered booklet that had obviously been around and waved it.

"You name a place, and we'll go."

"I will right after you take care of this." She rummaged in the purse some more before pulling out a chunk of stone, jagged on one side but smooth on the other three.

"What is that?"

"As if you can't guess," she teased, handing it over.

I stared at the broken tablet, the writing etched into it. "Is that the prophecy? But you said you didn't have it."

She smiled at me. "I never said I didn't find it. Everyone assumed I hadn't since I didn't give it to Lucifer."

"Why didn't you?"

"For one, it's incomplete."

I glanced at the broken tablet, and my brow furrowed as I did my best to translate. What I read didn't appear good. "Probably a good thing you didn't show the big boss."

"Exactly my thought. And I don't think a certain goddess should see this either," Dottie added.

"What do you want me to do with it?"

"Hide it."

She didn't mention destroying it, which I appreciated. All knowledge should be protected.

"I know just the place, but it will be tough getting there."

"I'm not afraid of danger."

I drew her close. "What if I told you that what we're about to do makes you an honorary librarian? And did you know I have a fantasy about that?"

"You do?" she said, her voice dropping down to a husky whisper.

I bit her lower lip and said, "I don't suppose you have a pair of glasses in that bag?"

She did. And the whole librarian thing was even better in person.

EPILOGUE

SHAX AND DOTTIE: A STORY OF SECOND CHANCES.

OUR STORY DIDN'T END the day we declared our love, it only began. Together, we were going to fill the pages of our lives. Embark on a journey, two perfectly matched—

"Whoa, Mr. Fancy Pants. This is some tripe. Where's the action?" Dottie stopped reading to shake the sheaf of paper at Shax.

"I'm getting there. First, I need to set the scene."

"I've got a scene for you. The head librarian, a handsome man with a lickable body, hears a giggle from between the stacks. A man of action, he pulls out his mighty lasso and races to find the invader. The lovely sea witch he finds cowering—"

"Cowering?" he interrupted. "Let's be honest. You never cower."

Dottie's lips curved. "True. Very well, the

gorgeous witch is waiting for him, beckoning. But he knows she is dangerous."

"So dangerous," Shax murmured pulling his witch close. "Which is why he loves her."

"And saves her from the goblin. EEK!" Dorothy darted out of reach just as the green ball of slime flew past.

Shax sighed and eyed the cock-blocking goblins. "You did not seriously do that."

"Kill it!" she screamed, standing on top of a table because that would make a difference.

"It's only a goblin."

"I wasn't talking about the goblin. I was talking about that!" She pointed to a place behind him.

Shax eyed the tree comprised of paper mache with branches made up of tightly rolled paper, lumbering toward them.

Every so often, the arts and crafts section went rogue and sent out monstrous creations.

Shax smiled. "Welcome to Hell's library." Where literature truly came to life.

THE SHIP MADE IT TO PORT WITH MOST OF THE passengers it had left with. Adexios was shocked.

The crew high-fived. No one noticed the shadow on the hull.

A thing accidentally brought back when a certain witch had brazenly used a living creature to scry. The rip in space and time proved large enough to let *it* through.

It was a small enough shadow that everyone ignored it. A good thing with it so weak.

It would hide until it had a chance to grow.

And then...every shadow wants to rule the world.

LUCIFER PUT THE PROPHECY FROM ATLANTIS INTO THE vault. No one would ever see it. Ever. Even Shax and Dorothy never even suspected it existed because he'd had them looking elsewhere.

No one could ever know about this possible future. He didn't dare tell even Gaia. Not now. Not ever.

A sound from the carpet where he'd placed his son brought him closer, forming a shadow over the wiggly bundle. Big eyes with hints of flame in the irises peered back.

Damian reached, two chubby arms and an eager

expression even the devil couldn't resist. He scooped the child up.

The baby patted Lucifer's cheeks. "Da 'kay?"

"Yes, Daddy is okay. Weren't you watching? That cruise was a new record for me." He'd matched thirteen couples on that trip. The most ever. "A good thing because he needed his minions reproducing. The legions would need more recruits before the prophecies began to play out.

Before the most important one came true.

"Ma?" Damian queried.

Lucifer sighed. "Your mum will be fine." Not a complete lie. Nothing would happen quite yet. But the ball had been set into motion.

Lucifer had accidentally impregnated Gaia. With a girl who, according to the prophecy, would become the new Mother Earth. But Gaia was too intricately wound around the planet to ever abdicate. Which meant the child she carried might one day kill her.

Lucifer loved his wife, but he'd always had a soft spot for baby girls.

And prophecies promising destruction.

WILL THE *SUSHI LOVER* EMBARK ON ANOTHER CRUISE?

What is that shadow planning? And how will Muriel handle not being Daddy's baby girl anymore? Find out soon as Welcome to Hell spins off into a new, exciting series: **GRIM DATING.**

Death has never been sexier.

Find out more at EveLanglais.com.

Made in the USA
Las Vegas, NV
17 July 2021